# THE HEIRESS AND THE BOY NEXT DOOR

## A SWEET WESTERN HISTORICAL ROMANCE

# RANEÉ S. CLARK

# CHAPTER I

*Northeastern Wyoming, June 1924*

Despite its ostentatiousness, Rosaline loved the brick Victorian mansion that looked so out of place on the dusty ranch. Grandfather and Grandmother had lived in a one-room cabin until he could erect the "proper house" Grandfather had promised to build when they'd left New York. And when he had, gosh darn, he'd built a proper house. He'd found the tallest hill he could and put the sixteen-room masterpiece right at the top. By the next summer, the sloping lawn and pine-tree-lined drive and grounds had rivaled any grand estate back east.

The music of those pine trees sang Rosaline to sleep more nights than not. When the Wyoming wind blew through them—and in Wyoming, the wind always blew—it sounded like a rushing creek. Like the sound of the mountains. Like a lullaby that soothed and told her she was home.

Rosaline looked up at the pale blue sky from her spot on the thick grass and grinned, until her mother's car rolled to a stop next to her.

"Better get on up and in, Miss Rozzy." The driver—and butler, and stable hand, and anything else he was called upon to be—quirked an eyebrow and wrinkled his forehead. It was a look he and Rozzy shared when her mother demanded something.

"Robert!" A light voice that stung with ice rang from inside the midnight-blue Rolls-Royce limousine Grandfather had arranged to be shipped from England the summer before. Bert insisted he had half a mind to drive the car into the ditch, considering the steering wheel was on the wrong side. Well, that and the fact that he was missing three of the fingers on his left hand. But the same war that had taken those fingers had made him one of the best men of all trades for miles around.

He exited the car and swept his hat off in an exaggerated bow. "Pardon me, Miss *Rosaline*."

Rozzy dropped into the pompous curtsy her mother taught her to execute perfectly. The blades of grass tickled her nose, she bent so low. Then she stuffed a giggle away and pranced to the car. Bert opened the door for her before getting back in.

"That's enough, Rosaline," her mother said, eyes narrowed at the high tilt of Rozzy's nose. "What were you doing lying in the grass? You've probably gotten grass stains all over your skirt." She inspected the tiered ruffles on the drop-waist skirt of Rozzy's dress, moving aside the maroon velveteen coat, its lining matching the geometric pattern of the dress, to inspect for damage. She sighed, in either defeat or disapproval, when she found nothing, and resigned herself to glaring in displeasure.

Rozzy straightened her hat and leaned against the seat. "It's the best spring day so far. I couldn't waste it inside the house."

"And a stroll would be too suitable for a hoyden like you?"

"Yes. Entirely too suitable."

"Good heavens, Rosaline, I'd send you out east to a proper school if I didn't think you'd embarrass us all with your antics." Matilda Pender rolled her eyes and pointed her gaze out the window. Her simple dark green dress didn't have a wrinkle in sight. Of course, she had been educated in an age when dresses had far more fabric to consider.

"I think that time has come and gone, Mother, considering I'm nearly twenty."

"It is never too late to learn good manners."

"I have excellent manners. Everyone says so."

"Robert and your father are not everyone, and neither are reliable authorities on manners."

Rozzy gave up on an argument she would never win. Grandmother had insisted that Mother be trained as well as any other debutante out east, and since Grandfather never denied either of his girls anything, Mother had spent years being educated among the best New York City could offer. Rosaline had rejected the idea, and they'd compromised with an excellent governess who had left two years before.

"Where are we going?" Rozzy asked.

"Mrs. Plummer sent a note that she'd gotten some new silk. I think we ought to choose something for your new dress."

Rozzy stared blankly at Mother for several seconds, trying to recall what she'd need a new dress for.

"The Roseboom wedding, Rosaline," Mother reminded her.

"I don't need a new dress for that."

"Indulge me, please. I'm sure Mrs. Plummer would appreciate the business."

Considering Mrs. Plummer was the best seamstress in town, everyone had probably ordered from her, and she would more likely appreciate Mother not adding another order to that. But one look at Mother's wistful face cut off any more of Rozzy's protests. Mother would have liked to live in New York City. The Nickels' wealth seemed wasted so far from the best society, with only a few wealthy families around and hardly any social events to speak of. Love had kept Mother in Little River, first for Rozzy's father and now for Rozzy—since Rozzy wanted nothing more than to die on the Arrow C ranch.

They spent the remainder of the ride into town in silence. Rozzy watched the sagebrush-covered expanse roll by until it turned into farms the closer they got to Little River, and then sturdy brick buildings when they joined the moderate bustle of cars, wagons, and even carriages of Little River's main street. Visits to bigger cities always proved to Rozzy how modern life was there, and perhaps she found it a bit of a comfort to come home to find Little River always a smidge behind.

Bert pulled up in front of Mrs. Plummer's shop, then hopped out to open their door and help them out. A loud whistle greeted them the moment Rozzy's feet touched the sidewalk. She looked up and grinned. "Daddy!" To placate Mother, whose face was already drawn into a disapproving frown, Rozzy kept a sedate, if not a touch hurried, ladylike pace as she moved to greet her father. When she reached the barrel-chested man, she wrapped her arms around his waist and pressed her cheek against his chest, taking one long, deep breath of his campfire-and-sweaty-man scent before pulling away.

By then, Mother had reached them. "Thomas Jefferson Pender, that is no way to greet a lady." By the pinch of her lips and the slant of her eyebrows, Rozzy knew that if Mother could have reached, she would have grabbed his ear and given him a good lecture. Not that anyone, least of all her father and his foreman Curly, thought it would do the great T.J. Pender any good.

Daddy put his hands on his thighs and let out a whistle loud enough to summon his old hounds from his shabby homestead on the edge of the Nickel ranch. Biting her lip to keep back a laugh at his antics, Rozzy glanced sideways at Mother. She had her hands on her ears and her lips pressed into an even harder line. By the twitch in them, Rozzy suspected she had a hard time keeping back her laugh. Sure, Mother and Daddy fought like two old badgers and hadn't lived in the same house for ten years, but he'd always known how to irritate her into a smile. And when he hadn't annoyed her for a while, Mother would mention that she'd fallen for that fool because he made her laugh so much she couldn't see straight—at least not straight enough to have the sense to accept one of the half dozen offers she'd gotten from rich gentlemen out east. In this day and age, Rozzy wasn't quite sure why Mother didn't divorce him and marry one of those dandies that came to visit the ranch every so often.

Daddy reached over and tilted up Mother's chin. "Aw, come on now, Matty. If you laughed every once in a while, you wouldn't have to walk with your nose so high in an effort to keep it all locked in."

Mother swatted his hand away as the blush rose to her cheeks. "That's enough."

His eyes dancing, he turned his attention to Rozzy. He pushed back his sagging cowboy hat to reveal a tuft of black and gray hair and bent to kiss her cheek. "How's my Rozzy?"

"Perfect, now that I've seen you. How are your sheep?"

"Rosaline, T.J. Her name is Rosaline."

Just like Daddy worked his way under her skin, Mother found her ways too. He always seemed to get the better of her, though. He scooped a hand around Mother's waist and pulled her next to him. "I ought ta know, shouldn't I? Since I picked out her name."

Mother struggled away, pushing against his chest and not gaining an inch. "Let me go. Let me go now. The whole town is watching you."

Daddy laughed, a deep chuckle that made most women in Little River shiver with jealousy. "And what will they wag their tongues about? Me kissing my wife?" He let her go, and Mother put plenty of distance between them, her face bright red as he kept on laughing.

She marched into Mrs. Gibson's shop, and Rozzy had no choice but to follow. She gave her father a peck on the cheek. "Aw, Daddy, you shouldn't do that to her."

He still couldn't suppress a smile, but he gave an honest effort at looking guilty. "I know, baby girl." He shooed her inside the shop, knowing she'd placate Mother better than anyone.

Rozzy had never wondered why Daddy didn't divorce Mother. He teased her because he loved her. It wasn't right, the way he needled her just to get her attention. It was a foolish way to win her attention, and Rozzy wished he'd see it. But he loved her. She knew that. His lips would sometimes turn down in sadness when he watched her, leaning toward her like he meant to stop her from walking away—again. But how many times had she heard him say that Mother expected too much of him?

It turned out that Rozzy didn't need to do any placating. Mrs. Gibson had pulled out the pale pink silk embroidered with tiny flowers in a shade just a touch deeper than the pink. Mother was already rubbing it gently between her fingers, oohing and ahhing over the intricate design. For the remainder of their several-hours-long visit—or so it seemed—Rozzy painted a complacent smile on her lips, nodded, and murmured, "Mmm-hmm," whenever the older women seemed to require her opinion, which wasn't often.

By the time they exited the store and woke Bert up to drive them home, Mother sighed and went on so much about how perfect Rozzy's dress would be, she seemed to have forgotten the incident with Daddy in front of the shop.

"Good afternoon, ladies!"

The familiar voice—not her father's, thankfully, though she loved this voice almost as much—brought a genuine smile to Rozzy's lips. And not just because it meant a few minutes conversing with Rafe Adams, but because Mother *adored* Rafe Adams. She thought him the best young man in Little River. If Rozzy was lucky, and if Rafe, though many years Mother's junior, charmed her as usual, Rozzy wouldn't have to hear even the slightest rant about Daddy's lack of character and proper gentlemanly behavior. Instead, her mother might only call upon her to support a mild tribute to Rafe, which she could always do and add plenty of her own compliments as well. On this point, she and her mother agreed. Rafe *was* the best man in Little River and Rozzy's very best friend.

"Well, hello, Rafe." Mother hung out her hand.

Rafe swept off his clean black cowboy hat and grabbed up her hand for a moment before turning his dimpled, choir-boy smile on Rozzy. "Mrs. Pender," he said quickly before taking up Rozzy's hand and holding it several moments longer than he had Mother's. "Miss Rozzy." He didn't care about manners. He knew enough to please Mother, but he wouldn't get offended if Rozzy didn't pay him the proper respect.

Though she scolded everyone under the sun for not using Rozzy's full name, Mother only cast an indulgent smile on Rafe. "He's known you all your life, after all," she'd told Rozzy once. "Since you were still in the cradle." As if Daddy and Bert and Curly hadn't either.

"Good afternoon, Rafe." Rozzy smiled.

"Are you gonna let Miss Rozzy come down to T.J.'s barn for the dance?" Rafe stood close to Rozzy, but he glanced at Mother when asking.

Mother's nose crinkled at being reminded about Daddy. Rozzy wished Rafe could have left him out of it. Mother had planned on going all week—for all her properness, she didn't mind a party with almost anyone in Little River—but her encounter with Daddy might have changed her mind.

"Of course we're going," Rozzy said before Mother could make any excuse about it. "We wouldn't miss it. Everyone's been talking about it forever."

"You'll both save a dance for me, won't you?" Rafe asked.

"Of course." Mother laughed, a sweet bell-like laugh that must have garnered a lot of attention in her day. She flirted so well. No wonder it disappointed her that she somehow hadn't passed on the trait and Rozzy cared more about learning how to run Grandfather's ranch so she could take it over some day. When she got a husband, of course. Her grandfather, Papa Ed, insisted on that. Probably because Mother did.

"I'd love to, Rafe," Rozzy said, practicing a sweet smile. Daddy had asked her to placate Mother. He'd want a dance with Mother too, and that meant buttering her up. Rozzy did want to dance with Rafe. He was the handsomest man in Little River, hands down. Well, besides her father, but of course he didn't count. If she didn't care so much about Rafe, she might convince him to marry her so she could get the ranch. But she couldn't inflict that kind of misery on her dearest friend.

There was Henry Granger to think of, too. There had been an understanding between them for years, arranged by their mothers. Rozzy had never objected. She needed a husband for the ranch, and Henry's lack of interest in her ranch made him the perfect option. The last thing she needed was some man sweeping in and taking over the work she'd dreamed of doing all her life.

"I hate to leave you ladies, but I have an appointment with the barber. Have to look my best tonight." Rafe smiled his dimpled smile again and bowed, waving his hat as he walked away before slapping it back on his head again.

Bert still waited at the door of the car. Mother took his hand and got in, waiting for Rozzy to do the same before she spoke. "Now *he* would make a good husband, my dear."

Rozzy ignored her mother's insinuation, as usual. "Is that a slight to Henry?" she asked with her pretended innocence.

Mother waved her hand in a dismissive gesture. "Of course not. He will also make a fine husband. But don't you like Rafe, dear?" Mother asked.

"Of course I like Rafe. I like him very much. Besides Papa Ed, he's taught me the most about how to run a ranch. He's my best friend in the world." She gave her mother a wide smile to chase away any romantic ideas.

Mother sighed in defeat and shook her head as the car pulled away from Mrs. Gibson's. "Yes, Rafe could run the Arrow C very well, couldn't he?"

"Rafe Adams has his own ranch," Rozzy snapped, scowling at her mother. "He doesn't need mine."

Mother didn't open her eyes. She laughed softly. "Yes, yes. But I'm sure it would ease Big Ed's mind if you were to choose Rafe instead. Someday you might want to do something more than ranch."

And Henry wouldn't know the first thing to do. Which was why Rozzy *wouldn't* choose Rafe. It might ease her grandfather's mind, but it didn't ease Rozzy's. She did not intend to ever give up her ranch to anyone, even Rafe.

"I doubt it would ease Papa Ed's mind much if Rafe's daddy got a hand on the Arrow C," Rozzy pointed out. She hated bringing Rafe's scoundrel of a father into this—heaven knew her friend wasn't a lick like him—but for the safety of her ranch, she had to do it.

It did the trick. Mother dropped the subject. She didn't like the thought of Papa Ed passing the Arrow C on to Rozzy, but he didn't have a choice. Daddy was a homesteader. He didn't have the blood of a rancher, and he didn't want it. He'd said so whenever Mother had tried to make him into what she pictured as the perfect gentleman cowboy. The Arrow C ran thick in Rozzy's blood. She *did* want it.

She wanted to ride over the miles and miles of sagebrush and wake up every morning with the mountains in the distance out her window. She wanted to hear the cattle and smell the hay. She wanted to feel the wind whipping at her hair before she stuffed it under the beat-up hat Grandfather had given her when she'd turned ten. That hat finally fit her, just like someday the Arrow C would finally be hers.

# CHAPTER 2

The sounds of fiddles and guitars had led Rafe Adams and his foreman, Jim McMullin, through the warm, late June evening to the worn barn next to T.J. Pender's one-room cabin on his homestead. Not that Rafe needed directions. The Pender barn had hosted more than its share of get-togethers for the settlers of Little River since the community had come together to build it two years after T.J. arrived and staked his claim. Because everyone liked the loud, boisterous, joking cowboy.

Rafe pulled the truck up next to the Nickels' fancy limousine and a handful of other cars, as well as some horses tied nearby and a few wagons. He and Jim strode to the large, open door of the barn, where light and music spilled out, along with a few couples hand in hand for a stroll around T.J.'s property. No big pine trees to hide them here. It always struck Rafe how different T.J.'s house was from Big Ed's. That's what everyone around called T.J.'s father-in-law, Edwin Nickel. T.J.'s place was just a cabin with a dirt roof and a barn already worn from too much snow and too much wind. All of it sitting in the middle of nothing.

Rafe followed Jim into the barn, like usual, even though now that he and his brothers had convinced their father to leave the running of the

Double A to Rafe, he was the boss. The Double A was biggest in the county after the Arrow C. Not as much of an accomplishment now that farming seemed to have taken over, but Rafe had always been proud of his place and grateful it had survived his father's stewardship.

He spotted Rozzy dancing with T.J. She missed half the steps and laughed over it. Rafe didn't need to look over at Mrs. Pender to know she cringed at every one. Poor Mrs. Pender. She wanted so badly for Rozzy to be a proper lady, had begged and begged for her to go get some polish in New York, like Mrs. Pender and Big Ed's wife, Mrs. Nickel, before her. Rafe always thought Mrs. Pender seemed a bit torn between her love for flashy society and her love of Wyoming, her father, and even T.J.

Jim hesitated inside the door to survey the scene, so Rafe took the moment to survey Rozzy. Her blond curls swung around behind her as T.J. twirled her this way and that, neither of them paying mind to the proper steps anymore. The hairstyle was a compromise, Rafe assumed, at Mrs. Pender's insistence. Whenever he rode with Rozzy on their ranches, she let her hair hang down straight under her hat, and Mrs. Pender would have preferred that Rozzy do something fancy, like the way several of the ladies had theirs waved close to their face and twisted at the back.

"Didn't your mother ever teach you that it isn't polite to stare?" Jim broke Rafe's reverie.

Rafe folded his arms and smiled but didn't take his eyes off Rozzy. "Doesn't she look just like a thunderstorm?"

Jim quirked an eyebrow and rubbed his chin. "I'm certain I can't follow that bit of bad poetry, boss."

Rafe chuckled. He never got the words quite right, but it wouldn't stop him from trying. Rozzy always laughed at him too, but he could tell she appreciated his musings even so. "Beautiful and terrifying all at the same time."

Jim shook his head. "Terrifying? Miss Rozzy? I think you mean Mrs. Pender, don't you? Miss Rozzy's as soft as a kitten."

"Mmmm. Nope. She's something fierce, as fierce as her mother, though she doesn't show her claws as much."

"Maybe terrifying to you." Jim slapped him on the shoulder. "There ain't nothing to be afraid of about Miss Rozzy, boss. Go on over there and ask her to dance. Ask her to marry ya, while yer at it, and do us all some good."

Rafe chuckled again and shook his head. "Not yet, anyway. Gotta talk her out of marrying that city boy first." Jim scoffed, clearly agreeing with Rafe on how likely it was that Rozzy would ever go through with her "engagement."

"Didn't you promise me a dance, Mr. Adams?" Mrs. Pender strode up to both men, nodding a greeting when Jim tipped his hat.

Rafe grinned. "I did." He straightened and offered her a hand to lead her into the couples.

"Hopefully you dance the foxtrot better than T.J." She rolled her eyes.

"I am known for being a mite better than T.J. at dancing, ma'am." He took Mrs. Pender's hand and rested another on her waist, waiting a beat before taking the first slow step forward.

Mrs. Pender beamed at him as he guided her in the quick step before moving forward again. "You really are a treasure, Mr. Adams," she praised him when he smoothly executed the rock step to make a turn.

Without breaking step, he grinned and bobbed his head. "Thank you, ma'am." Now if only her daughter admired his fine dancing as much.

It didn't surprise Rafe one bit when a particular turn led them near T.J. and Rozzy, or that T.J. took one look at Rafe's partner and stopped them. "Now, don't be offended, Rozzy, but I think I'd prefer to finish this foxtrot with Matty. She seems to dance much better than you."

Rozzy laughed at him and put her hands on her hips. "Well, she should. She was trained by the best dance masters New York City has to offer."

T.J. shook his head at Mrs. Pender. "Don't I know it? It was the longest five years of my life." He reached for her hand. "May I have the honor?"

"If Rafe wasn't dying to have a dance with Rosaline, I wouldn't pay you any mind."

"Don't be a tease, Mrs. Pender. You know you can't help but pay me mind."

"You're an incorrigible flirt."

"I think since I am married to you, it's allowed."

Both Rozzy and Rafe laughed at her parents' arguing as they moved away, T.J.'s steps perfect now that he had his Matty in his arms. "I think he might like her better than me," Rozzy mused, tapping a finger to her lips before turning to Rafe with a grin. "Stubborn pair."

"I know a girl just like them."

She scowled at his insinuation. Though he knew the steps well enough not to make a misstep, he didn't turn as much as he should for the promenade step and let his leg brush Rozzy's as he stepped across with his right foot. "You do not," she protested. She didn't react in the slightest to their touch, as usual. He wondered if she ever felt the electricity cracking like a whip between them as he did.

"She's also rather sweet, so that makes up for it."

She turned a soft smile up at him, and in moments like that, he wondered if she might feel an inkling of something for him. "That's better."

When it came to Rozzy, there was one thing Rafe excelled at as much as he did wrangling cows: inching her closer to him without her realizing. Of course, it wasn't all that hard. Rozzy was so oblivious to any attempts he made to flirt that he could have branded his cows with Rafe + Rozzy = and she would have missed it. He still enjoyed the occasional time she would rest her cheek on his shoulder and the way her sweet rose scent drifted up to him.

The tune picked up too soon for him, but he was a quick stepper and had Rozzy laughing as he twirled her around. He couldn't keep her all to himself for long, though. When the guitars had stopped strumming and before they wound up for the next song, one of his own ranch hands hurried over to ask Rozzy for a dance.

But when she'd danced with her share of other partners, and Rafe saw his first chance to intervene before another eager young Little River man beat him to her, he scrambled across the room. "Take a walk with me, Rozzy?" he asked with his best charming smile.

Rozzy's pretty pink cheeks, glowing from not sitting even one dance out, complemented the beautiful gray green of her eyes as she smiled at him. "Oh yes, I'd really like that." She took his arm until they reached the big barn door, where Rafe took her hand in his.

And she let him, like she always did, though she thought of it as an act of friendship rather than something more. She liked him, he knew that, but they'd spent so much time together as friends and working side by side that she only saw the rancher in him, the teacher, the one who'd help her out when Big Ed passed the reins of Arrow C on to her. And he had to consider that blasted understanding between her and Henry Granger. At least she never expressed any feelings of affection for Henry.

Rafe and Rozzy walked along the fence line until they put a big enough gap between them and the closest couple. When they stopped, Rozzy leaned against the fence post and stared across the landscape before tipping her head back as far as it would go to examine the sky.

"They don't ever get old, do they?" she said. "All those stars."

Rafe sat on the top rail and lifted his legs to rest on the bottom before following her gaze. "Nope," he agreed. He'd lain awake staring at them enough times when they drove the cattle into the mountains for summer range. Still, the sight of all those tiny white lights—sometimes so many they cast a faint white stain in the sky—surrounded by the deepest shade of navy always made him a bit speechless.

They'd settled into silence for so long that Rozzy's voice startled Rafe. "You know something, Rafe?"

"Huh?"

She didn't notice his lack of attention. Her eyes were roving the landscape again, on one side the Arrow C and on the other the Double A. T.J.'s homestead was the only thing that separated the boundaries of the Double A and the Arrow C. "Sometimes I feel like the Arrow C is sewn into my soul. Like I couldn't rip it out if I tried." She sighed and rested her chin in her hands.

One corner of his lip came up. He tried all the time to say things like that on purpose, and it never sounded as nice as it did coming from Rozzy. "I like the way you said that."

Her gaze swung to him, and she tilted her head to rest against his arm. "Did you? Nothing as pretty as the things you say."

Rafe let his hand run over her curls before he rested it on her shoulder. Darn it, he wanted to kiss those perfect pink lips. Nigh on a year had passed since he'd snuck his last kiss from her—an innocent peck on the cheek. They weren't kids anymore, and when Rafe did start courting her, after convincing her to forget about Granger, he wanted her to know he was serious, not playing games. Though he was only four years older, he'd looked out for Rozzy since she was born, more so since T.J. had moved off the ranch and back to his homestead ten years ago. Rafe had ridden up and down the Arrow C with her, teaching her when Big Ed couldn't, showing her the ropes. Everyone in town knew Rozzy was his sweetheart—everyone, it seemed, but Rozzy.

Rozzy broke the silence again. (Of course, it would please Rafe very much to sit and stare at her all night without saying a word.) "Mother and Daddy seemed a little bit happy tonight, didn't they?"

Rafe didn't miss the longing in her voice. He didn't care if he spoke the truth or not. He said what she wanted to hear. "They did. T.J. didn't hardly dance with anyone else."

She hoisted herself up to sit next to him. "Sometimes I wish Daddy would just move back up to the ranch." She rested her head on his shoulder now. It made Rafe afraid to breathe—made him want to wrap her in his arms and steal that kiss, no matter the risk.

"Just sometimes?" he managed to tease her instead.

"He needs to be who he is. Mother wants to make him into a gentleman, like Grandfather. I don't think she realizes she wouldn't love him as much if he was who she wanted him to be."

Rafe ran his hand up and down her shoulder. "He could try. For her." He meant the words to comfort. They'd talked about her parents many times over the years, had this conversation many times. Rafe always thought the same thing. If T.J. *really* loved Mrs. Pender, he'd do what it took. And from what he could tell, he did *really* love her. Rafe would never understand it.

"He did before, you know. When he lived at home. It wasn't enough for her."

"Give them a few more years."

Rozzy laughed and looked up at him. "Okay. A few more years." She chuckled to herself again. "Why would anyone do that to themselves?"

"Do what?" Rafe asked.

"Rosaline? Is that you?"

Rafe turned to see Mrs. Pender making her way across the field toward them, scattering couples in her wake.

Rozzy straightened but didn't put any distance between her and Rafe. Mrs. Pender had never been strict when it came to Rafe's attentions to her daughter. "Yes, Mother?"

"Oh . . ." Mrs. Pender halted her advance, worry disappearing from her expression and melting into a knowing smile. *If only*, Rafe thought. Still, ever the dutiful mother, Mrs. Pender said the proper thing. "Don't you think you ought to come inside before people start to talk?"

Rozzy waved her off. "Oh, Mother, it's just Rafe. Everyone already talks about us anyhow."

Mrs. Pender shook her head. "Well, it wouldn't be fair to Henry if he were to hear such talk." Rafe didn't miss that Mrs. Pender's voice lacked the concern she lectured Rozzy over—one of the prime reasons Rafe didn't put much stock in the understanding between her and Granger.

"I doubt anyone in Denver cares for gossip in Little River," Rozzy huffed.

Rafe slid off the fence. "Don't tease your mother," he said, offering her his hand. She hopped down and took it. "That's T.J.'s job," he whispered, making her giggle.

When they got back to the barn, he led Rozzy out for a dance. Someday he'd do what Jim had said and propose to her, see what this irresistible girl had to say about that. But that would have to wait until he knew that she'd say yes.

Matilda Nickel Pender's insistence that her daughter obey the rules of propriety had Rafe taking a turn with one of the Anderson girls instead of spending the entire night twirling Rozzy around the faded planks of the barn's floor. But since he almost always had her in his sights, he noticed when she abandoned her dance with the sheriff's deputy mid-Charleston to rush over to her parents.

Public displays of *dis*affection were not uncommon for Matty and T.J. Pender, even during the days of their wedded bliss, and neither were their daughter's attempts to stem them. Like one of his cows drawn to the only bit of grass in a dusty field, Rafe excused himself to help her out, arriving at Rozzy's side in time to hear T.J. say, "Aw, heck, Matty. Either you wanna be my wife or you don't. Unless you're goin' to come home, I'm rather tired of your hissy fits over my flirting."

Not only did Mrs. Pender's face go a deep shade of scarlet, but so did Miss Maggie's, the town librarian who stood behind T.J.'s shoulder and who was the most likely target of whatever flirting T.J. defended himself against.

Mrs. Pender focused her glare on T.J. "If I recall correctly—and I always recall correctly—I was not the one to leave."

Rozzy grabbed Rafe's arm and pulled him forward. She hadn't turned to see him, so how she knew he stood there was beyond him. Of course, he always stood at the ready for Rozzy. "Oh, Mother," she said. "Look. Here's Rafe. He dances the Charleston so well. Wouldn't you like to dance it with him?"

"You go on ahead," Mrs. Pender said with a sideways glance at him. The fact that she hadn't spoken in that normal uppity way of hers clued Rafe in on her setting up to lecture T.J.

"It woulda been awful hard for me to leave *you,* seeing as how you never lived in my home." T.J. jerked a thumb in the direction of his shack.

Mrs. Pender let out a bark of incredulous laughter. "Can two people actually occupy that . . . structure at the same time?"

T.J. leaned forward, his face a breath from Mrs. Pender's. "Perhaps we ought to go an' test that theory out, darlin'."

She balled up one of her fists, and Rafe stepped in before she threw a punch that would break her lovely fingers as well as T.J.'s nose—and not for the first time, either. Despite her eastern education, Mrs. Pender was still a ranch girl.

"Mrs. Pender, I'd be very obliged if you'd dance the Charleston with me. The song's near over, so we ought to hurry." Rafe slipped his arm through hers, nudging her away from T.J.

"I . . . well . . ." Mrs. Pender began, but the farther Rafe got her from T.J., the less she struggled. A few steps from the dance floor, all the righteous indignation had left her, but one glance said that it was taking refuge in some angry tears gathering in her eyes. "On second thought, Rafe, it's getting quite late. Perhaps you'll find Robert for me and have him get my car ready."

"Yes, ma'am." Rafe nodded and caught Rozzy's face falling. "If Rozzy would like to stay, I'd be glad to see her home."

"Oh, would that be okay, Mother? Or would you like the company on the drive back?" Rozzy chewed on her lip, waiting on Mrs. Pender's answer. She was likely to say no just because it meant Rozzy spending time alone with a young man and no chaperone.

"Is that proper?" Mrs. Pender asked with an arch of her brows, but Rafe thought there might be more calculation in that expression than shock.

"Oh, Mother." Rozzy folded her arms and threw her mother a scowl. "We've known Rafe forever, and it's such a short ride."

"Just because you live among ruffians doesn't mean I will consent to your wholeheartedly embracing their ways," Mrs. Pender said tartly.

"Yes, Mother." Rozzy's shoulder's drooped, as did Rafe's hopes for another dance or two with her.

"But I don't suppose it would be too bad if Rafe saw you home." Mrs. Pender smiled at Rafe, her preference for him winning out, despite the friendship she shared with Granger's mother. "My car?"

"Oh, of course." Rafe darted away. He frowned over the fact that T.J. had gone and asked Miss Maggie to dance with him. Hopefully Rozzy'd had the good sense to walk her mother to the barn door.

"Smartest cowboy from here to Denver," he muttered to Bert when he caught up with the Nickels' man of all trades. "Doesn't know a lick about women."

Bert looked over Rafe's head and rolled his eyes. "Should I get the car?"

Rafe nodded. "Mrs. Pender's ready to go."

Bert acquiesced with a nod of his own and pushed his way through the cowboys he'd been mingling with to head out for the Nickels' car. Since it was one of only a handful of cars at the event, by the time Rafe met the ladies in front of the barn, Bert was already pulling it forward.

Rafe handed Mrs. Pender into the car. "You'll behave properly toward my daughter, won't you, Rafe?" she asked.

He cast her a reassuring smile. He didn't remind Mrs. Pender of the many times he and Rozzy had ridden fence lines by themselves, Rafe teaching her the ropes of ranching. But ever since her debut ball when Rozzy had turned eighteen, Mrs. Pender had made it clear that their "friendly" terms of childhood would come to an end and that if Rafe meant to pursue her, he ought to go about things in the proper way.

"Have I ever treated her anything but?" he teased.

Mrs. Pender cast him a wry, but affectionate smile. "Not recently, anyway." She let go of his hand and settled back into the seat. Sometimes Rafe understood how difficult it must be for T.J. to love her. She was such a confusing mix of women—one who longed for the glitter of her own ballroom days, for high society and strict, proper etiquette. Layered in with that was a tough woman who'd grown up on a rough Wyoming ranch and weathered her own share of hard times. And somewhere underneath lay a kind, passionate matriarch who'd taken to mothering Rafe when he needed it.

He stepped back, and a moment later, Bert rumbled the car forward over the rocky ground between the barn and the road that led out to the Nickel place.

# CHAPTER 3

Without Mother to go on and on about how many dances it was proper to dance with a gentleman, Rozzy accepted more than one additional invitation from Rafe to dance—but not enough to make people talk. That would get back to Mother. As silly as she thought her mother's lectures on propriety were, Rozzy despised sitting through them. She avoided those lectures by trying her hardest to live up to them. Maybe it was Daddy's independent streak running through her that made her fail more often than not.

Besides, people would talk about her and Rafe anyway. They always had. And they wouldn't stop until one or both of them got married. That's how folks were. But just when Rozzy thought she might regret marrying Henry instead of Rafe, like tonight when they'd looked up at the stars together, her parents reminded her how messy love was. Too bad married life couldn't be more like her relationship with Rafe now—simple, affectionate, and sweet. She hoped to put off marrying Henry for a few more years, but when she did, it would be a partnership between friends. Two people who wouldn't make each other miserable with heartache like her parents did. She didn't care for Henry the same way she did Rafe, but that was the point. Less suffering for all concerned.

What kind of girl would Rafe marry? It didn't surprise Rozzy that the thought brought more than a twinge of jealousy. She'd been the "only girl for Rafe" (his exact words) for as long as she could remember. Seeing as how his mother had been dead for almost six years, for a while now Rozzy had been the most important woman in his life. She didn't relish giving up that position.

"What kind of girl do you suppose you'll marry?" she asked out loud as Rafe led her to his truck. His foreman, Jim, had stayed behind with some of the other cowboys—hands that the Arrow C, the Double A, and Daddy had hired on, or men and boys who came through and worked other farms in the area.

Something like fright flitted across Rafe's face before he chuckled. Rozzy scanned the darkened ground, looking for a mouse. Silly as she'd always thought it, the only thing that struck fear into Rafe Adams was mice. She'd once watched him unload a six-shooter trying to kill a rodent they'd come across on the range.

Rafe opened the door for her and handed her into the truck, which felt ridiculous, considering the truck was more utilitarian than anything else. He closed the door and hurried around to get in, starting the engine as he said, "I've been thinking about marrying an heiress." He winked. "One with a lot of land and a fine spread of cattle. Know any girls like that?" He pulled away from the barn, which still played host to a lively party, even so late into the night.

"None willing to give up their land to a husband," she shot back with a teasing smile of her own.

"I suppose I'll have to settle for you, then, Roz." He tipped his cowboy hat in that "handsomest man in Little River" way of his.

A giggle escaped her. She did love the way he could make her laugh. "Be serious, Rafe," she insisted. Enough people gossiped about Rafe being sweet on her that the first person she needed to convince that she wouldn't marry him was Rafe himself.

"I am." He wiggled his eyebrows at her, and she knew he wouldn't answer seriously. What if he married some girl he'd known back in his college days at Purdue? Or maybe his brothers had someone in mind for him up in Cheyenne. Rozzy hated the thought of not knowing.

"You know, at least Mother cares enough about Daddy to wish he'd quit flirting. That's something, don't you think?" she said after a few moments of comfortable silence.

"Sure is," he agreed. He reached over and took her hand. It was a habit since childhood and his way of comforting her. She gripped it hard. She didn't want to think about how they had grown up and would soon have to leave their days of friendship behind, and the more she allowed him to do things like this, the more he'd keep on hoping.

They couldn't stay best friends forever, even if Rozzy wouldn't mind that. She could run the Arrow C, and he could run the Double A—but maybe she would get lonely without a husband. She knew Mother was. It haunted her eyes, like tonight when Mother had seen Daddy saying things that made Miss Maggie blush, just before the anger at him acting that way with her only standing a few feet away took over.

They reached the fork in the road where the lane to the right would take a traveler to Rafe's house and the lane to the left would take one to the Nickels' home. Rafe slowed the truck to turn left, but Rozzy sat up. "How are the puppies doing?" she asked. "I can't believe I haven't been down to see them. Can we go now?"

"Roz, it's past midnight. Your mother would skin me." But he pressed on the brake and brought the truck to a complete stop.

"She'll be in bed by now. I'm sure her argument with Daddy gave her a headache. She won't know the difference of half an hour." She flashed him a pleading smile. "Oh, please, Rafe. I'll bet they're the sweetest little things."

Rafe rubbed the back of his neck. "Half an hour," he repeated, attempting to sound stern, which made Rozzy swallow back a giggle.

He turned and took them down the road to the Double A. He parked the truck in front of the barn, and he and Rozzy hopped out. Once inside, she grabbed a lantern from a hook nearby, lit it, and hurried toward the corner where she heard the puppies whining.

"Well, they sound adorable . . . and hungry," she said, crouching down. The small balls of yellow fur, golden like their mama, rolled around Queenie, sucking on her teats for a few seconds each before being nudged aside by a sibling and squealing some more. "Rafe, what's wrong with them?" Rozzy crouched lower, her brows furrowed with worry. The more she listened, the more she believed their high-pitched yips sounded troubled.

Rafe took the lantern from her and held it at Queenie's head. Her eyes were closed, and she flinched every time a puppy latched on. "I don't think they're getting any milk." He softly rubbed the top of his dog's head. "What's wrong, girl?" he whispered.

"We need to get these puppies some milk before they all die of starvation." Rozzy picked one up and offered it her finger, which the pup sucked on, but it whined when it received nothing.

"I'm afraid you're right. I'll get some and be right back."

Rafe took the lantern with him, but enough moonlight shone through the window nearby that Rozzy could make out the shapes of the six puppies and their ill mama. She gathered the puppies into her arms, stroking the tiny things and whispering reassurances about how she and Rafe would get them some food as soon as they could.

Rafe hurried back with a pail of milk and a few tin cups. "Dip your finger in and let them suck it off," he instructed as he poured her a cupful and handed it over. He poured his own and reached for three of the puppies, settling them in his lap as he sat cross-legged. The puppies yelped with glee at the change of their circumstances, and Rozzy couldn't help laughing at the eager way they slurped at her fingers.

"What do you think is wrong with Queenie?" she asked, when she and the puppies she held had gotten into a rhythm and the poor things acted less starved.

"Don't know," Rafe replied. "I'll send someone for Dr. Anderson tomorrow and have him come out and look at her."

"I hope it's nothing serious."

"Me too."

Rozzy frowned in concern. Though his father had conned Queenie away from one of the neighboring farmers, the puppy had trailed Rafe around the ranch from the get-go. When Rafe had heard about how his father had gotten the dog, he'd tried to return her to old Mr. Stewart, but the man complained that Queenie whined two nights in a row for Rafe after being returned and he couldn't stand it anymore. Rafe ended up scraping together all the money his teenage self could, coming over to the

Arrow C to work for Big Ed after his work at the Double A was done so he could pay Mr. Stewart the high cost of the purebred lab. He loved Queenie like one of his siblings, and if something happened to her, it would kill him.

It took some time—time that Rozzy lost track of—but finally the puppies were satisfied, and she settled them on her chest and leaned back into some nearby hay, her shoulder pressed up against Rafe's. She smiled at the way the puppies breathed in their steady rhythm and how silky their new fur felt. Soon her own eyes drooped. She'd close them for a second while Rafe finished feeding his puppies . . .

"WELL, WELL, WELL." A voice startled Rozzy awake. "What have we got here?"

Her eyes snapped open to see Jim standing above her, lit up in the pink light of the rising sun coming through the barn door. "Puppies," she said with a yawn. "Hungry ones. Something's wrong with Queenie, and she's not giving any milk." She slipped out from under Rafe's arm, which had somehow come around her after she'd fallen asleep. She blushed, avoiding Jim's gaze as she realized she had slept with her cheek against Rafe's chest.

Rafe stirred at her movement but didn't sit up until Jim nudged him with the tip of his boot. Jim crouched over Queenie himself. "What's the matter, girl?" he crooned.

"Good heavens, what time is it, Jim?" Rafe asked, sliding the puppies on his chest into the bed next to Queenie.

"Dawn, boss. Should be obvious." Jim chuckled.

"Rozzy, your mother is going to shoot me. Come on, get up now." He reached for her hand, and she struggled to transfer the puppies in her lap to Jim as Rafe hauled her up.

"Now, Rafe. I'm sure she'll understand." She quirked an eyebrow at him.

"Your mother? No, she won't," he insisted. "Jim, send to town for Dr. Anderson and get someone to come in here and help you feed those puppies again. I'm gonna drive Rozzy home."

"Yes, sir," Jim said, laying the puppies in with Queenie and striding out the door behind the couple.

The entire three-mile drive home, Rafe kept taking off his hat and wiping his brow with his sleeve, sweating like it was the middle of July. He would ruin his good shirt. He already had dirty puppy prints up the front of the white button-down and across his brown trousers.

"Really, Rafe. I think you're worried about nothing." Rozzy tried to soothe him, but the truth was, his worry worried her.

"Perhaps you've forgotten who your mother is," he said, rubbing at his cheeks with one hand. A light scruff of blond hair had started growing on his chin. He didn't bother shaving much when he rode the range day after day, but when he got dressed up for parties like the barn dance last night, he always shaved. He was quite attractive, she realized, and that twinge of jealousy came back. Some girl might snatch him up quicker than Rozzy was comfortable with. And she couldn't help that waking up in his arms would stay with her for some time. His clean, musky scent still lingered in her memory, as did the warmth of his arm on hers where her short sleeve hadn't covered. The heat in her cheeks returned, and she ducked her head to hide it.

"She might be strict, but she's fair," Rozzy insisted, hoping her voice didn't betray her. "She'll understand about the puppies."

Rafe huffed in response. Neither of them spoke the rest of the way. He brought the truck to a skidding stop in front of the house, sending dirt and pebbles flying. Before Rozzy could even react, he hopped out, ran around, and opened her door.

The front door of the house flew open as they hit the steps, and Mother stepped out onto the porch in her dressing gown, her eyes flaming like a bonfire. "Where have you two been?" she cried.

"Now, Mother, I was helping Rafe feed Queenie's puppies. Looks like something's wrong with her and—"

"You spent the night with Rafe in the barn at the Double A?" Mother's eyes bulged, and she put a hand to her heart.

"Let me explain." Rozzy held up her hands as she came forward, wishing her mother didn't have such a quick temper. "Something's wrong with Queenie, and the puppies aren't getting any milk."

"Rozzy—!" The use of her shortened name by the woman who had scarce let that nickname pass her lips made Rozzy understand Rafe's sweating. "That is no excuse for spending the night in a barn with a gentleman. At least, I *thought* he was a gentleman." Mother turned her glare on Rafe. A lesser man might have turned to dust under such scrutiny as Mother could dole out. Looking close, slim ribbons of smoke seemed to waft off him. Perhaps it was just some swirling dust from their quick stop, but it made for a disturbing image.

Rozzy took in a deep breath. "Mother, it's not as bad as it sounds—"

"It's exactly as bad as it sounds," Mother snapped. "Do you know what people will say? Did you agree to this, Rafe? Didn't you promise to treat my daughter properly?"

"Yes, ma'am." Rafe cleared his throat again. Rozzy wondered which question he was answering. "But you see, in the heat of the moment, I could only think of saving the puppies . . ." He trailed off when the continued widening of Mother's eyes made it clear the puppy explanation made no difference to her.

She turned immediately back on Rozzy. "Rosaline Pender, people in Little River look to our family to set the example of propriety—" Rozzy held back a snort of laughter while Mother continued. "—and by noon tomorrow, everyone will have heard that you two were doing who knows what all night in the Adams barn. And make no mistake—that news will make its way to Denver."

"Mother!" Rozzy would laugh if humiliation hadn't choked that notion down. Humiliation and worry over what Henry's mother would say and what kind of pressure she would put on Henry over it. "We were not doing who knows what. We were feeding puppies."

Mother pinched her lips so tight they puckered.

"I think you're overreacting," Rozzy went on in a soothing tone.

"Overreacting? To my daughter's honor being besmirched by the one young man I trusted to take care of her?"

Rozzy hoped her blush didn't give away the reminder that she'd woken with Rafe's arms around her. Of course, it had been innocent, but it likely didn't look so. "Mother, it was nothing like that, and people wouldn't dare talk. No one would think that of Rafe," she protested.

"He has a bunkhouse full of hands that would dare talk and won't mind spreading indecent things about an heiress like you." Mother spun back to Rafe. "Mr. Adams, call upon me tomorrow, and we can discuss the consequences of your actions."

"Yes, ma'am." Rafe made a quick tip of his hat toward Mother but didn't dare move yet.

"Rosaline, come inside before matters get worse." Mother turned on her heel and headed for the front door.

"I'll talk some sense into her," Rozzy whispered to Rafe before skedaddling up the steps to follow her mother inside. She didn't know what Mother was so worked up about. Maybe if they lived in New York, where folks didn't know their neighbors from Adam, but not out here where everybody knew everybody else. They trusted each other, and Mother should especially trust Rafe. He'd never given any reason for anyone to believe he'd behave anything but gentlemanly. If Henry did hear of the incident, Rozzy was sure a simple talking-to would put things right.

"Good day, Rozzy." Rafe tipped his hat at her and gave her his choir-boy smile—forced—before he hurried around the truck and hopped in, roaring away without a backwards glance. She wouldn't mind watching him drive down the road, wishing she was going off with him somewhere to work on the ranch, but Mother had been serious about her getting inside.

Mother waited in the hallway outside the front parlor. "You treated Rafe awful hard, Mother," Rozzy said.

Mother clenched her jaw. "Rosaline Pender, you've done some foolish things, and I don't care where we live—I raised you to be a lady. Ladies *do not* spend the night with a man." She held up a hand to stop Rozzy's instant protest. "Not even one you've known all your life. Not even to save his puppies. Even if I know I can trust Rafe Adams."

"It sure didn't sound like it." Rozzy crossed her arms and stared her mother down. She'd learned a thing or two about that stare in her almost twenty years. She hated to think of Rafe worrying over what Mother thought, and worry he would.

"Rafe knows better," Mother snapped. "I know he's been more like a brother to you than anything since you were a girl, but that's changing. You have to accept it. People around here may tolerate lax manners in society, but if you give them one reason to doubt your morality, they will turn on you like wildfire, even in the middle of nowhere in Wyoming."

Rozzy swallowed her protests at the anger in Mother's eyes. Mother had weathered her share of rumors since Daddy left, and Rozzy had to agree that her good breeding had kept her coming out on top of them every time. "I'm sorry, Mother," she said. She only felt a smidge of it, but it would get her out of this lecture quicker by saying it.

Mother let loose a deep sigh and reached for Rozzy's hand. "You're not twelve anymore. People have talked about you and Rafe for years, yes, but that talk will change if they hear about last night."

Heat beat in Rozzy's cheeks at even the thought of her mother being right. "Yes, Mother."

Mother leaned in and kissed Rosaline on the cheek. "Go up to bed, dear. We'll figure this out later when we've both had some more rest."

# CHAPTER 4

When Rafe arrived at the Nickel residence the next day at the appropriate time for afternoon calls, the housekeeper, Mrs. Hewitt, led him back to Big Ed's study. Even though it was empty, it banished the somewhat good humor Rafe had arrived in. He'd trusted that Rozzy could calm her mother down and convince her that what had happened was a foolish, innocent mistake that neither would repeat. He'd expected a warm welcome into the family parlor, where he was usually received, but if Mrs. Pender wanted to see him in Big Ed's study, she must still mean business about whatever consequences the events of last night might hold.

She came in a few minutes after Rafe arrived. "Good afternoon, Mr. Adams," she said with a pleasant, but stiff smile. "Would you like anything to drink?" She held out her hand to one of the chairs along the wall opposite Big Ed's large, ornately carved desk. Rafe dropped into it with a shake of his head, and Mrs. Pender took a seat behind the desk. That made his shoulders tense. How official.

"I would like to apologize again for my lack of judgment, Mrs. Pender," he offered, sweeping a hand over his still-wet hair. He'd come in early from the range to clean up and make himself presentable, since Mrs. Pender would expect that of a proper caller. And to get back in her good graces, he had better do the proper thing. She was stuck in some old ways, and he wanted more than anything for her to think highly of him. Mrs. Pender might hold some extra affection for him, but in the department of proving worthy of her daughter, he had to compete with the polished manners of Henry Granger.

"Thank you, Mr. Adams." Mrs. Pender folded her hands into her lap. Rafe wished she'd stop this "Mr. Adams" business. Another practice she'd started after Rozzy's debut, and the formality of it made him uncomfortable. "I think Rosaline's growing up has somewhat surprised us all. It may be a difficult transition for us to treat her as the lady she's become."

Despite not being sure if Rozzy would ever turn into the lady Mrs. Pender wanted her to become, he nodded. "I promise not to forget that again."

"I don't suppose you will. What did your cowhands have to say about last night?" She quirked her eyebrow enough to convey that she knew she'd guessed correctly about their assumptions.

Rafe had taken a ribbing—not the kind that any of them would repeat in front of Mrs. Pender or the ladies she associated with, but enough to make him realize his gaffe was genuine. Jim had made one comment, a slip in his teasing about how Rafe's arm had wound around Rozzy, that the men had picked up and made sound scandalous. They were a rough crowd, and he had a few on hand for the summer who he didn't know as well as he should. Word, embellished even, might get around despite his efforts to curb the rumors.

"What you thought they might, ma'am." Heat filled his face.

"I hope, Mr. Adams, that you are honorable enough to do what is required when a lady's reputation may be compromised." Mrs. Pender leaned forward, fixing her sharp eyes on him.

It took a moment for Rafe's cowboy mind to untangle her hoity-toity way of speaking, but the implication hit him hard when he did. "I . . . well . . . I would never dream of . . ." But none of the words tumbling around in his head made it out of his mouth. He took a deep breath. For a long time, Rafe had wanted Mrs. Pender to believe him worthy of marrying her only daughter, a daughter for whom she had dreamed of making the best match possible. A match to defy the dismal state of her own marriage. Rafe had worried more than once that when he convinced Rozzy to marry him instead of Henry, Mrs. Pender would reject the choice because he was a cowboy, and despite the impressive suit he would make in being the owner of the Double A, she might not think him much better than the cowboy she'd married and lost faith in.

"And Henry Granger?" he questioned in a hoarse voice. He didn't know if it would disappoint Rozzy or not if her understanding with Granger was dissolved. She hardly spoke of the man to Rafe, making it easy for him to undermine Granger.

Mrs. Pender's jaw tensed. "Rosaline phoned this morning, believing she ought to warn him rather than have him find out from gossip that will be inflated." Her fingers tapped out an impatient rhythm on top of the desk, her tone disapproving. "Though Mr. Granger did nothing drastic as of yet, I expect his mother will insist he break things off once she is apprised. Her notions of propriety are far stricter than my own." She took a deep breath. "And once that has happened, Rosaline's reputation will suffer." She arched a brow, indicating that was where Rafe came in—to save it.

He replied with absolute honesty, considering the situation. "You know, ma'am, that I'd like nothing better than to make Roz—Rosaline my wife, but I can't force her to accept me, and I'd hate to think that's what it would take to get her to marry me."

Mrs. Pender coughed suddenly into her handkerchief. A strange reaction, he thought. But she leaned forward further, her expression as stern as ever. "Would you rather that Little River—and those of her acquaintance in Denver, I'm sure—tear her reputation to shreds?" she asked. "As I told Rosaline last night, she's no longer a girl and people may soon be hard-pressed to think her antics with you 'cute' any longer. You know as well as I that while it may be your cowhands talking right now, it won't be just them for long. I won't allow this town to gossip about her the way they have me."

"I won't have that either, Mrs. Pender." His response came automatically. He'd fight everyone in town to keep Rozzy's reputation intact. Heavens, he'd gladly marry her to do it too.

Mrs. Pender reached forward and pressed on a button that rang for the housekeeper. "I trust you'll do the right thing." She sat back, clasping her hands in front of her demurely as she stared at him from behind Big Ed's enormous desk. It reminded him of a picture he'd once seen at Purdue of Queen Victoria. Not that Matilda Pender looked anything like Queen Victoria, but she stared at him in the same imperious way the young queen had from the image of the painting.

Before Rafe could respond to what, in essence, equaled a command to propose to Rozzy, the door opened and Mrs. Hewitt, the housekeeper, entered. At first, relief washed over him that Mrs. Pender simply intended to ask for some refreshment despite him turning it down earlier. He could use a cold lemonade—or something stronger. If Big Ed had been around, Rafe felt sure the man would have seen to that in short order.

However, Mrs. Hewitt stood aside as she ushered Rozzy into the room, her eyes wide and filling with confusion when she met Rafe's gaze. She wore a plain navy skirt with two lines of embroidery down the front, and a loose white sweater with a string of pearls. Somehow Mrs. Pender had forced her into proper afternoon-caller clothing as well.

Did Mrs. Pender intend for him to offer marriage right here? In the study? Sweat beaded along his forehead. He'd had much more romantic plans for declaring his love for Rozzy. He always thought he'd propose quietly with just the two of them, out on a ride. He'd planned on asking Mrs. Pender's and Big Ed's permission beforehand—going about it the proper way that Mrs. Pender insisted on. He supposed he'd forfeited that when he'd fallen asleep in the barn with Rozzy in his arms.

Rozzy's expression collapsed into one of compassion as she rushed across the room to her mother. Mrs. Hewitt closed the door behind her, but not before casting her own look of compassion at Rafe.

"Oh, Mother," Rozzy cried. "Have you been lecturing Rafe about last night? I promised, didn't I, that it wouldn't happen again. We understand, Mother. It was foolish and thoughtless—and oh, won't you just leave Rafe alone. He's sweating something fierce—"

"Hush, Rosaline," Mrs. Pender said sternly. "Clearly everything I said has gone in one ear and out the other, since that is no way to greet a gentleman who has come to call upon you."

Rozzy straightened up and turned slowly to eye Rafe. After a long moment where confusion filtered back into her expression, she came forward and stiffly held out a hand to him. "Good afternoon, Rafe—"

"Mr. Adams," Mrs. Pender corrected.

"Now really—"

"Mr. Adams," Mrs. Pender insisted through clenched teeth.

Rozzy closed her eyes and drew in a breath before opening them and allowing Rafe to glimpse the mirth building up despite the strange circumstances. Would she laugh if she knew what was coming? Would she accept it?

Would she have accepted him had he not participated in compromising her character?

"Good afternoon, *Mr. Adams*," Rozzy said, even dipping into a slight curtsy.

"Good afternoon, Miss Pender." Rafe would like to laugh at himself for calling Rozzy "Miss Pender"—the girl who had once given him the silent treatment for a straight week when he'd told her he was going to Indiana to go to college. He'd had to promise to write her once a week for it to end. She'd been a kid then, though. She likely wouldn't force the same sort of promise now.

Rozzy swept out an elegant hand to gesture toward the seat he'd stood from when she'd entered. "Won't you take a seat, Mr. Adams? Perhaps Mother would ring for some tea or lemonade."

"Er . . . yes, perhaps—in a moment, Roz—I mean, Miss Pender. There's something I've got to say first." He cleared his throat and gripped her hand—tighter than he should have, considering the alarm that dashed through her expression. He loosened up but didn't let go. He'd planned on proposing to Rozzy for years now. He shouldn't let these blasted nerves twist up his gut like a knotted rope.

He dropped down to one knee before his fear got the better of him. Rozzy's eyebrows shot up like a yearling colt not yet trained and trying to buck off a rider.

"Miss Rosaline Pender, would you do me the honor of being my wife?" It came from his mouth so fast he prayed she'd understand, because heaven help him, he didn't think he could repeat it.

Rozzy's mouth dropped into a pretty little *o*, and her free hand rose to cover it. Rafe held his breath, pleading with his eyes for her to relieve the sharp pains slicing through his chest right now—fear that she'd reject him. Despite the circumstances, he'd never wanted anything more than this girl to be his. More than he'd wanted to go to college at Purdue, and he'd had to leave Rozzy to do that, so it really said something.

He swallowed. "Please, Roz," he said, his voice low and husky.

Rozzy's eyebrows lowered, shrouding her eyes with the same bewilderment that had plagued her from the moment she'd entered the room. She tilted her head at him, and then her breath caught. Her eyes widened, and she spun away from him. "You!" she cried, yanking her hand from Rafe's to point an accusing finger at Mrs. Pender.

Mrs. Pender had her hand over her heart, and her eyes looked a bit misty. The next moment, she scowled at Rozzy. But before she could form a stern reply, her daughter went on.

"How could you do such a thing? You've made my dearest friend in all the world propose to me over something as silly as accidentally falling asleep in a barn, when in fact we've been alone all night many times when some ranch emergency called for it and everyone in town knows it."

"I assure you, Rosaline, that Mr. Adams is in earnest." She gestured to Rafe, who scrambled up from where he was still kneeling on the floor. He should take some relief from the fact that at least someone in the room knew him well.

Rozzy didn't bother even turning to inspect if this was true or not. With a sinking heart, Rafe realized he didn't know if he could ever convince her that while Mrs. Pender had insisted on the timing, she hadn't forced the genuine feelings.

"Of course he's in earnest—what have you threatened him with?" Rozzy demanded.

"Rosaline Pender, mind yourself," Mrs. Pender said in a shrill voice.

Two bright spots of red burned in Rozzy's cheeks when she whirled back on Rafe. "No, *Mr. Adams*, I will not accept your kind offer of marriage to save my reputation, no matter what horrible punishment my mother has pressured you wi—"

"ROSALINE PENDER."

Unaffected by Mrs. Pender's outburst, Rozzy grabbed up Rafe's hands in hers. "You're my best friend, Rafe," she said, her eyes sparkling with genuine feeling that ripped straight through him. *Best friend.* "I couldn't force you to take me as your wife, even if the whole town is wagging their tongues about us by nightfall." She dropped his hands, straightened her shoulders, and tipped up her chin in defiance. "I'm prepared for the worst."

"Even Mr. Granger's impending desertion?" Mrs. Pender snapped.

Rozzy blanched but gave a tight nod.

"Rozzy," he said in a low voice. "My feelings for you are quite genuine."

"Oh, Rafe. I know you'd do anything for me, even marry me, to keep me from being talked about, but the storm shall pass. I might even still make a smart match to some fellow from out east who doesn't know about my—" She dropped her voice to a scandalized whisper. "—*reputation.* Surely silly gossip can't spread that far." She winked, and Rafe had to swallow a laugh. Otherwise he might cry from disappointment, hardened cowboy though he was.

He turned his gaze to Mrs. Pender, pleading for . . . help? Forgiveness? Mrs. Pender had one hand shielding her eyes, exasperation hanging over her entire expression. "Well." He worried the edge of his hat and then plopped it on his head. "If that's your final answer, Miss Pender—" He hoped he was acting as casual about the whole thing as her, especially considering it felt like someone had lassoed his chest and was squeezing the life right out of him.

Rozzy giggled, then clapped a hand over her mouth.

"Good day," he choked out. Saying anything more would give him away. He bowed his head to them both and shot for the door, swinging it open to find Mrs. Hewitt waiting, a hopeful smile ready. It fell the moment he met her eye. Tipping his hat, he hurried past her and out of the house.

# CHAPTER 5

"Why do you keep checking that pocket watch, Johnny?" Rozzy snapped at the twelve-year-old Cowles boy. His mother was Rafe's cook, but the boy did work for both ranches to supplement the widow's income, and right now he rode alongside her over the brush-covered ground as Rozzy checked on their cattle herds. She studied the herd in front of her as she waited for his answer, watching for any signs of injured or sick cattle.

"Mrs. Pender said I ought to make sure yer home in time to get ready for Miss Van Doren's tea party," he said, tucking the watch back into the pocket of his trousers. He had told her last week that the dinged-up, dingy golden contraption had belonged to his father and Mrs. Cowles had given it to Johnny for his birthday. If there was anyone Mother could have trusted to make sure that Rozzy got back to the ranch house in time to make herself presentable for a trip to town, it was Johnny.

Rozzy sighed and nudged her horse to move quicker than she wanted. She could use a good long ride over her land to remind her that all this fuss was worth hanging on to marrying Henry so she could keep the ranch and not hand it off to some man—even if that man was Rafe. Her gaze caught on a cow lying down, and she nudged her horse in that direction. Before she'd made it more than a few steps, it stood and wandered closer to some other cows to munch on some grass.

"And how much time have we got?" she asked Johnny, softening her voice. She hadn't meant to be so harsh, but after the last few days of hullabaloo, her patience wore thinner than a banjo string.

"Ten minutes, miss. Just enough time to get back to the house." He nudged his own horse into a trot to outpace Rozzy's.

"I'm going to brave Mother's wrath to check on a few cows that Ray said he saw heading for this draw." She pointed to the gap between two large hills, covered in pine trees, that rose up before them.

Johnny nodded and consulted his pocket watch once more, pressing his lips into a firm line. Rozzy held back a laugh at his concentration and the calculations he must be making in his head. When he looked up, she shot a grin at him and spurred her horse, Irene, to a gallop toward the mouth of the draw. A small creek ran through it, which made it a popular place among the cattle to come to graze, and sure enough, about a hundred head lazed along the edge of the creek, calves nestled up beside their mothers as they rested in the tall brush. She and Johnny did a quick count of the calves, tossing numbers back and forth to each other until they had a good idea of how many.

A loud, mournful moo called Rozzy's attention farther up the draw, where sloughing off the bed of the creek had created a sharp drop of ten or so feet on either side. As she came up to it, she caught sight of a cow lowing in troubled tones over a calf stuck deep in the mud on the far side of the creek. Rozzy slid off her horse.

"You ain't got time, miss!" Johnny called to her. "I'll go get Ray. I saw him working on some fence a few miles back."

"This'll just take a few minutes," she said. "But go ahead and go after Ray in case the calf is deeper than I think." She waved Johnny away as she splashed through the water.

"Mrs. Pender won't like this," Johnny said, but he turned his horse and trotted off.

Mrs. Pender might not, but Rozzy couldn't help herself. The sad cries of the calf reminded her of the sweet puppies, which hardened her resolve to busy herself with ranch work.

As her mother had warned, Henry had called yesterday to inform her that his mother insisted he sever their connection. Her own mother had lectured Rozzy nonstop ever since, going on and on about propriety, how she should have accepted Rafe, how much she must have hurt him turning down his proposal like that—trying to convince Rozzy he'd honestly wanted to marry her.

Rozzy threw her arm around the neck of the calf and dug her feet into the squishy mud. Of course, she knew Rafe had proposed in earnest, though she'd played the fool, like always. She yanked on the calf, her anger at her mother flaring again as Rozzy thought of the hurt she'd caught in Rafe's expression, the tightness to his farewell smile, and the way his fingers gripped the rim of his best hat. Her mother had made Rozzy do that to him—insisting she marry him! Why couldn't that woman, of all people, understand that Rozzy had no wish to be married, least of all to Rafe, who she loved more than almost anyone?

She gave a yelp as she slipped in the mud, landing hard on her back and feeling the muddy water seep into the back of her shirt. Oh, showing up at the ranch house late was sure to anger Mother now, since it might require a full bath. She stood up, laughing to herself and thinking what Rafe would say if he saw her.

She stopped the thought. Her feelings for Rafe . . . The fact that he always slipped into her mind somehow, a wish to be with him or a memory they shared—that was exactly the problem. Every once in a while, Mother would tell Rozzy stories about falling in love with Daddy, about the heartache from missing him that had plagued her while she'd lived back east, and about the way he'd made her heart leap with the touch of his hand, never mind how kissing him had flown her over the moon. When she talked about Daddy like that, her snooty way of speaking dropped away, and the cowgirl slipped out.

When Rafe had taken Rozzy's hand and said that sweet proposal, for one moment she'd understood the passion that had driven her mother to accept Daddy. That was a heap of trouble Rozzy didn't dare step in, one she wouldn't punish dear, good Rafe with either.

"You alright, Miss Pender?" Ray called from across the creek.

Rozzy snapped to attention, realizing she still sat in the mud petting the poor calf beside her. She gave a sigh and hauled herself up. "I guess I should have listened to Johnny and waited for you." She gestured to her muddied-up self.

The tall, middle-aged man chuckled as he moved his horse to the middle of the creek and tossed Rozzy a rope. Ray Eubank had worked for Papa Ed as long as she could remember. She tied the rope underneath the front legs and around the upper part of the calf before securing the knot and nodding for Ray to pull back. Within a few minutes, the calf frolicked away into the creek.

She caught Johnny checking his watch from behind Ray and laughed. She rinsed her hands off in the creek and hopped back up on her horse. "I know, I know!" she called to Johnny as she rode off.

Luckily, Mrs. Hewitt met Rozzy at the door. "Your mother has a headache and won't be going into town with you," she said, following Rozzy up the stairs.

"It's no wonder with all the lecturing she's been doing," Rozzy murmured. Mrs. Hewitt pretended not to hear and drew up a bath, letting Rozzy know she'd come back to do something with her hair afterward.

Later, when Mrs. Hewitt had hustled her out of the house and into the car, Rozzy leaned back against the seat of the Rolls with a sigh. Though she despised both social teas and Tillie Van Doren, the ride into town provided at least a moment of peace—especially without Mother along to lecture. A jolt nearly sent her sprawling onto the floor of the car, and she hurried to right herself. She pushed at the gauzy peach hat Mother had ordered from New York, hoping she hadn't squished it.

"Last week's rain sure did a number on this road," Bert said by way of apology.

"Yes, I see." Rozzy settled back in the seat again, this time bracing her hand against any more jolts. The next one might have the skirt of her drop-waisted, lace-and-silk tea dress up over her shoulders. Mother could only handle so much scandal. Rozzy showing her knees to Bert and the cows might put her over the edge once and for all.

Tillie's housekeeper led Rozzy into the parlor, which was old fashioned and crowded with what Little River had to offer for society ladies. Unfortunately, Tillie, with Bess Anderson on her heels, accosted Rozzy the moment she came in.

"Well, you'd better tell us right now, Rosaline Pender: when is the date?" Tillie demanded, reaching for Rosaline's hand and scowling over it.

Rozzy yanked it away. "What date?"

Bess rolled her eyes before glancing around the room. "No need to keep it from us, Rosaline. We know all about it. When are you getting married?"

Heat swept into Rozzy's cheeks faster than a March rainstorm could turn into snow. She squared her shoulders for the low gossip that Tillie and Bess were bound to spread about her. "I am not getting married over something so foolish."

Both Tillie's and Bess's mouths fell open. "He didn't offer." Tillie dropped her voice to a scandalized whisper.

Before Rozzy could get a word out, Bess said, "Well, of course he must not have, or Rosaline would be getting married—her mother would see to it. And it shocks me to the core, Tillie, I'll tell you. I thought Rafe Adams was the neatest boy in Little River. I can't believe he didn't ask you."

Rozzy's stomach turned into a boulder. She had been prepared to rebut any slights to her own character—which was what her mother seemed afraid of—but she hadn't expected anyone to speak so of Rafe. Why, he *was* the neatest boy in Little River. In all of Wyoming!

"Well, he must have heard that Henry Granger won't have her." Tillie shook her head in disgust. "To think that all these years we thought Rafe cared for you." Her disgust turned to shallow sympathy.

Oh, Rozzy couldn't stand to hear them talk about Rafe like that. "But he—"

"Oh, don't you worry, Rosaline." Tillie took back her hand and gripped it. "Your mother will find you someone right away and you won't be the worse for wear over it." Her eyes widened, and she leaned in. "You're not in the family way, are you?" She'd dropped her voice to a whisper, but Rosaline caught heads turning their direction anyway, and more than one pair of eyes widened in surprise.

"Good heavens, Tillie, we were feeding puppies!" Rozzy snapped. "Really. You're one to talk."

Tillie narrowed her eyes. "Feeding puppies?" And then she giggled and shared a look with Bess, who started giggling as well. "Everyone in town is saying you two must have been up to something. Good luck getting anyone to believe you weren't necking." With a swish of the lace on her skirt, Tillie and Bess slipped away arm in arm.

As Rozzy surveyed the room, she noted the whispers that had started and the shocked expressions on the faces of Mrs. Watson, the reverend's wife, and Mrs. Gifford, the banker's wife, whom Tillie and Bess had joined in conversation. Rozzy's chin began to tremble, but she shook her head. She would not let these ladies see any weakness in her.

She cornered Tillie before the tea was over, taking her by the arm and pulling her away from Bess Anderson.

"Goodness, Rosaline, what's gotten into you?" Tillie cried when they'd reached the hallway outside the Van Dorens' parlor. She shook Rozzy's hand off her arm.

"I had to get you to listen, Tillie," Rosaline said, moving to block Tillie's return to the parlor. "Rafe *did* propose to me."

Tillie stopped trying to get past Rosaline, and she smoothed out the wrinkle of confusion on her pert little nose. "If that's true, why aren't you marrying him?" She had softened her voice, but it came out as a challenge.

Rozzy squared her shoulders. "I turned him down."

Tillie laughed, but when Rozzy scowled at her, she choked it off. "Why in the world would you do such a thing? Rafe Adams is the best catch in town. There's not a girl on this green earth that would turn him down." She arched her eyebrow.

"Well, I did." Rozzy stood her ground. "The whole thing is a big misunderstanding, and only a bunch of stick-in-the-muds would insist that a girl has to get married because she fell asleep feeding some puppies."

Tillie didn't bother trying to hide her skeptical smirk. She stared at Rozzy, apparently waiting for her to come up with a better excuse.

"You have to help me, Tillie. Make sure people know he's a good, upright man."

Tillie snorted and gave a shrug. "I'll do what I can, but you know how people talk."

Rozzy attempted to sweeten her tone. "If anyone can convince people in town what truly happened, it's you, Tillie Van Doren."

She preened but didn't soften near enough for Rozzy's liking. "I can *try*," she said. "But if you wanted to save Rafe Adams's reputation, you'd quit making a stand for something ridiculous and marry him." She didn't wait for Rozzy to reply before she opened the door of the parlor and stepped inside.

Rozzy didn't know if she hated anything more than admitting her mother was right—especially in this situation—but she'd read the scorn and condescension in Tillie's expression. Rozzy wouldn't win any friends among the younger women of Little River for being daft enough, in their eyes, to turn down a proposal from the most eligible bachelor in town. Besides being mighty handsome, Rafe ran the Double A, an impressive spread of land.

It might be time to go back to him with her tail between her legs and accept that proposal. At least until she could figure out some way to get them out of this mess without Rafe getting the short end of the stick.

Of course, changing her mind and accepting Rafe wasn't as easy as she hoped. She had Bert drive her up to the Double A after she left Tillie's, but he wasn't there. His housekeeper didn't know where he'd gone off to either. Rozzy checked in the barn—and checked on the puppies as well. They were nestled contentedly against Queenie's side, all of them sleeping, so she left without disturbing them. To think such sweet, tiny puppies had caused such a big, tangled problem.

Bert drove her home, and she changed out of her nice tea dress and back into another set of riding clothes, since Mrs. Hewitt had taken the muddy trousers, button-up shirt, and handkerchief from this morning away to launder them. Outside on the porch, she knocked as much mud as she could off her cowboy boots and smashed her hat onto her hair, probably ruining the elaborate twist Mrs. Hewitt had done after her bath.

She didn't meet her mother as she left the house, and all the better. Rozzy could do without the dose of "I told you so." Since she'd told Bert she wanted to ride when he dropped her at her house, he had her horse ready when she came into the barn.

She took a moment to stroke Irene's neck and whisper to the beautiful, dark brown mare. She'd been a gift from Daddy several years before, and he had laughed at her naming such a high-spirited animal something as mundane as Irene. She mounted and trotted from the barn toward the Double A. Rafe could be anywhere, but Rozzy could use a good hard ride to clear her thoughts after butting heads with Tillie. Her and Bess's condescension still rang in Rozzy's ears, as well as the persistent hiss of whispers that had followed her through the tea.

Well over an hour later, she spotted Rafe riding along a fence line alone. She spurred Irene toward him. It took a few moments for him to notice the noise, but he looked up, put a hand over his eyes, and squinted at her. She didn't miss that he took his hat off and wiped at his brow before he slapped it back on. He avoided her gaze for the few minutes it took her to meet him.

"Hello, Rafe."

"Good afternoon, Miss Pender," he said.

Rozzy waited for the quirk of his lips and his half-hidden smile to follow his greeting, but it didn't. He stared down at his saddle horn and wouldn't meet her eyes. "This isn't my mother's parlor. You're allowed to call me Rozzy out here, same as you always have."

He lifted his head and studied her, squinting his eyes against the sun—she thought. He had a peculiar look on his face. "All right," he said in a resigned tone.

Rozzy's heart twisted. He must have heard some whispers around town too, and perhaps her refusal had stung more than she figured. She should have thought about that before she'd selfishly declared that she'd face any gossip Little River had to offer. The men probably weren't as subtle about their judgments as the women.

"Well, it will come as no surprise to you that I've been proven wrong in my assessment of how the people of Little River would react to my lapse in judgment concerning the puppies the other night." Rozzy looked past Rafe as she spoke, the same heat that had blazed through her at the tea taking over her face now.

"Aw, you know I can't regret you asking to see them, Roz," he said, sounding more like himself but still not looking at her. "You likely saved their lives."

Rozzy caught on to the topic for the time being, turning Irene to fall into step alongside Rafe as he continued his ride along the fence. "Is Queenie going to be okay, then?"

"Yes. The vet said it's an uncommon condition that causes a fever and the milk to stop. So we'll have to feed them from now on. Queenie can't feed them anymore."

"I'd like to come and help—not in the middle of the night, of course, but sometime during the day."

"I'm sure Mrs. Cowles would be glad for the help."

They rode on in silence while Rozzy worked up the courage to speak again on the subject she'd come out to broach. "Rafe?" She cleared her throat, and he looked up at her, meeting her eyes for a moment before looking away again. "It seems I was quite hasty in declining your, er, offer earlier this week."

Rafe's shoulders tightened, and he sat straighter in his saddle. "I figured your mother'd send you on over before too long."

Rozzy slumped, hating the disappointment cutting through his tone. Of all the rotten things, to have their friendship ruined in one stroke like this—a silly misunderstanding and a wedding of all things. She didn't know if she could ever forgive Mother for making Rafe propose. It had made Rozzy face up to painful things long before she wanted to.

Something wiggled in her stomach at those thoughts. Maybe it wasn't fair to blame her mother so much. Everyone in town had expected Rafe to propose, and if Mother hadn't pushed it, the mess might be even bigger.

She huffed to herself. Still.

Before she made sure Rafe knew she could never marry him, she had to fix the mess she'd made. "It's just that people are talking, but not just about me, it seems. Truly, Rafe, it shocked me to discover it, but I can't bear it. Bess Anderson said she couldn't think you the neatest boy in Little River anymore for not behaving properly toward me—not that she gave me a minute to explain that I'd been the rash one to refuse you. I could tell them until I'm blue in the face, but Mother was right about how people will turn—Anyway, I can't have anyone saying things like that. Not about you." Her chin trembled again, but she didn't try to hide that from Rafe, not from her best friend in the whole world, before she ruined that by treating him so rotten. He'd seen her cry often enough not to be surprised. Before he'd gone off to college, tears had always been a cue for him to pull her into a hug and reassure her—when wolves had slaughtered several calves or when she'd wished Daddy would come home.

"And what did they say about you?" he asked, his jaw working.

Indignation burned in her stomach as she remembered what Tillie had asked her. She steeled herself against it, though. Folks always had plenty to say about the ranchers in the area. Not usually about their love lives, but if she was going to be as tough as Papa Ed, she had to get used to it. "I don't care what Tillie thinks about *me*—she really isn't one to talk, considering how she's always flirting with any boy who will have her, and we both saw her disappear with Danny Bridges the night of the dance. I bet they weren't feeding puppies," she snapped. "I can combat any nasty rumors she wants to make about me."

Rafe chuckled. "And I can't? I don't care what people think about me, neat or not."

"I won't stand it. What about when you decide to really get married, Rafe, to some sweet girl . . ." Rozzy trailed off at the familiar jolt that went through her when she pictured having to end their friendship on account of him getting married, but she had to be reasonable. He would someday, of course.

"I was under the impression that you'd come out to tell me you'd been hasty in rejecting me." Rafe sighed, and his tone had the same resignation as earlier.

"I did. I was. Let's tell everyone we're engaged, and I'll do something ridiculous like run off somewhere." She turned to Rafe and clasped her hands together, willing him to understand how she wished to save him —to save them both from themselves. "If I go see Henry, I'm sure I can convince him to elope with me or something." Though the fact that Henry Granger allowed his mother to lead him along, same as always, had put a mighty big wrench in things, it was the exact reason she'd entered into an understanding with him. He wasn't likely to try to boss her around. She'd make him see sense where it concerned her. Her money came with a lot more freedom than his mother's. So long as he didn't try and touch her ranch.

Rafe hung his head and laughed, his shoulders shaking. "You'd run off on me, would you, Roz? Make me the laughingstock instead of the villain?" He laughed a bit more and then shook his head at her. "It won't do. Mrs. Pender wants your reputation protected. You can't go creating another scandal."

"And you can't marry me just so people won't talk! It isn't right," Rozzy protested. "You've done nothing to deserve it."

"Haven't I?" he asked.

His tone struck her silent for a moment. She stared at him a good long time. "You don't deserve me," she said, her tone low. It was her turn to stare at her saddle horn. When she looked up, she caught him cringing and realized how it had sounded. "I mean, you deserve a whole lot *better*. Someone sweeter and maybe willing to keep house for you all proper, instead of running off to ride the range all the time." Not someone who didn't know the first thing about love thanks to her parents. Someone who couldn't tell the difference between passion and hate.

"And what would Mrs. Cowles do if I let someone get into her kitchen?" he asked.

Some of the knots broke up in her chest, and she cast him a grateful look as she laughed. "Maybe she'd find time to get a husband of her own."

Though his expression remained light, Rozzy didn't miss the sigh in his next words. "Well, the question remains, Miss Rosaline Pender: are you going to marry me or not?"

She had to save his reputation, one way or another, and for now, this seemed like the way. "I'll say I will, Mr. Adams." She gave him a determined nod. "But don't you worry. I'll find a way to get you out of it."

He turned his attention to the fence line, his tone empty. "I suspect you will."

# CHAPTER 6

Rising up early the next morning for branding helped relax some of the unease that had stayed with Rozzy after her conversation with Rafe. A day of hard work on the ranch would do her a world of good. She didn't bother Bert to get her horse for her, instead saddling Irene herself, like any other hand on the ranch. This early in the summer, the air held a chill that tickled over her cheeks. She tipped her hat back as she rode so she could study the mountains rising up blue in the distance. Soon they'd move the cows there to graze. She hoped her mother wouldn't keep her home this year with some notion of wedding preparations.

The crying and lowing of the cows and their calves greeted her as soon as she neared the corrals. Hundreds of calves filled the biggest pen, crying in protest at the cowhands riding through and roping them. Papa Ed sat on his horse at the head of the corral, watching over a dozen hands. As she passed the gate, one of the ropers tipped his hat at her as he dragged a calf out of the pen toward one of the fire pits.

"Morning, Papa!" she yelled when she'd reached Papa Ed.

"Morning, darlin'!" he shouted back.

She put a hand to her eyes as she surveyed the scene before her. "Didn't realize I'd slept in. You've already got all the cows cut out?"

Across the pen in the pasture, the mamas alternately chewed on the grass and mooed their protest to the treatment of their babies.

"Sure do."

She reached for her rope, tied behind her on the saddle. "I'll get to roping, then." Already her fingers tingled with the anticipation.

"Your mother would prefer you oversee." Papa pushed his hat back to wipe his brow on his sleeve.

"You're doing a fine job of that. Besides, you're getting too old to wrestle." She grinned wickedly as she moved her horse toward the gate of the pen.

Papa gave a loud guffaw and waved his hat at her. "I can still rope circles around you, darlin'!"

"Is that a challenge?" she called back, bringing her horse to a trot to return to the gate. The noise around them made it impossible to hear a reply, so Papa Ed replaced his hat and shook his head with a chuckle.

"Mornin', Miss Pender." Hank, one of the hands, tipped his hat as he passed her, dragging a roped calf over the grass-studded dirt, kicking up a swirl of dust behind him.

"Morning." She nodded back, suppressing the annoyance that they didn't treat her as one of them. Then again, if her mother caught any of them not giving her due respect, they'd be skinned alive, so Rozzy couldn't really blame them.

She pulled Irene to a stop at the gate and hung her rope on her saddle horn long enough to pull her gloves on. The whooping and yelling of the cowboys around her filled her ears as she spun the rope in her right hand, prepping to lasso one of the calves. The wiry threads of the rope tickled her exposed wrist as she twirled it.

She missed on her first toss, earning her some good-natured ribbing from the other two cowboys in the pen. She laughed along with them. As practiced as they were, they missed a few here and again as well. She caught the hind leg of a calf on her third toss. Making sure to secure her rope against her saddle horn, she headed out of the pen, scanning the area for an open fire pit. With so many calves, six fires were scattered around the huge pen, each busy as the men worked efficiently to move the calves through.

"Mornin', Miss." Ray Eubank raised a hand of greeting as she pulled the calf to a free pit.

"Morning, Ray." She waved back as he slipped the rope off the leg.

He and another hand secured the calf on the ground for the brander. She turned her horse to trot away. She never let on that she didn't relish the branding part. No rancher worth his salt had a tender heart over branding, but the smell of burning hair turned her stomach. She'd skipped breakfast to avoid an embarrassing repeat of when she was twelve and had lost her breakfast right after dropping off her first calf to the pit. She could stomach it if she had to and had once even insisted to have a turn at it so she could learn every part, but roping remained her favorite. She'd gotten good enough that no one ever questioned why she chose it every time.

Rafe had helped her practice, sacrificing his own limbs as she tossed at him time after time. She couldn't help smiling as she thought of him running around the yard in front of the house, waving his hat and taunting her.

She did glance back over her shoulder in time to see the cowboys release the calf to run to the pasture and perhaps find his mama. She let loose a deep, gratifying sigh. Then she picked up her rope and twirled it in the air. If only Rozzy could lasso up all the ugly gossip about Rafe. She'd have things fixed already.

# CHAPTER 7

Since Rozzy, in Mother's words, had "gone and made a proper mess of things," a formal engagement party was the way to solve it—that is, to make sure everyone who mattered in Little River knew well and good that Rafe Adams had proposed to Rosaline Pender and she had accepted.

Rozzy was subjected to having her waist-length hair finger-curled and twisted into such a mess she stared at it in horror for a solid two minutes before Mrs. Hewitt demanded what she'd done wrong.

"It's awful pretty," Rozzy said, turning her head this way and that, "but I do believe you will have to cut every lock off to get it out of that twist. Wherever did you learn such a thing?"

Mrs. Hewitt's shoulders relaxed, and she chuckled as she turned to pick up the dress she'd brought in for Rozzy to wear. "Oh my sweetheart, when I came here from England, it was as the right and proper lady's maid of a real English lady."

Rozzy could only stare at the gray-haired woman, hair pulled back into the simplest of buns, this woman who had rocked her and half raised her and run the Nickels' household for as long as Rozzy could remember. "Whatever are you doing in Wyoming?"

Mrs. Hewitt rolled her eyes and aimed a soft swat at Rozzy's backside. "Dearie, you are so much Edwin Nickel's daughter, I've begun to think you bleed Arrow C, but it's a shame you don't know anything of your family history. That proper English lady was your grandmother—youngest of six girls to a poor earl whose crumbling estate was entailed away to some distant cousin. Why, knowing that Big Ed could provide a comfortable home for his daughter was all Lord Norton asked for."

"You must be joking. If I was the granddaughter of a proper English lady, Mother would no doubt beat me over the head with it to shame me for my bad manners." Rozzy shook her head in disbelief.

"Oh, it's true, love. Get into this now. Your mother is right proud of it, for sure, but I dare say you wouldn't sit still long enough to hear something that didn't concern your precious ranch."

Shame trickled through Rozzy. Mrs. Hewitt did have a point. To think she'd come to almost twenty years old and never known about her grandmother's heritage. "Well, let's keep it our little secret that I know now, shouldn't we?" she said, feeling the heat of her embarrassment creeping up her neck. "We know I'll never hear the end of how I must have disappointed Grandmother or how her well-bred ancestors must be rolling in their graves to have a hoyden like me in the family line."

Mrs. Hewitt tsked as she helped Rozzy into the dress, a sleeveless shift dress with layers of rose-colored frills and a belt of fabric to tie at an angle at Rozzy's hips. As Mrs. Hewitt poked and prodded at her clothing, Rozzy pulled on her gloves, thinking of how overdone the whole thing was.

"There," Mrs. Hewitt said as she stood back to admire their handiwork. "You haven't done too bad, now, have you? Even for a hoyden." She winked and leaned forward to adjust a few of the wayward frills. "You're marrying the most eligible gentleman in Wyoming—besides Big Ed himself—I believe."

She beamed at Rozzy with such pride that Rozzy had to whirl around and make a pretense of preening in the mirror. But she struggled not to scowl at the lady in the mirror. She looked nothing like the woman who would someday run the Arrow C—Papa Ed's heir. No one would ever take her seriously as a rancher in getups like this.

"I suppose I'll do." She gave Mrs. Hewitt a little shrug, eliciting a look of confusion from the housekeeper, and then exited the room. She might as well get this circus over with. It was for Rafe's sake, in any case, and she could stand polite conversation and stuffy dancing for a few hours for him. She'd run amok in his life enough that he deserved for her to sacrifice in the name of his honor.

Rafe had thought the most exciting thing of the evening would have been Bert showing him into the ballroom of the Nickels' mansion and seeing T.J. Pender in a tuxedo, complete with a stiff collar that the old cowboy pulled at six times in the time it took Rafe to walk across the room to shake his hand. Rafe whistled lowly so Mrs. Pender wouldn't hear when he approached the old cowhand. T.J. and Mrs. Pender stood with Reverend Watson and his wife. "How did Mrs. Pender manage this marvel?" he asked with raised brows. "I reckon she must have roped and hogtied you to get you into that getup."

T.J. chuckled and tugged at his collar yet again. "In my dear wife's words, I have done enough in this lifetime to ruin my daughter's reputation. It's the least I can do to put on proper attire for one or two evenings and give her future nuptials the pomp they so deserve. And she would be right." He gave a decisive nod and cleared his throat.

Affection rose up in Rafe's chest for—well, he couldn't quite be called his future father-in-law, considering Rozzy planned on leaving him at the altar or some other crazy thing. He stuffed down his irritation at that. At Mrs. Pender's insistence—and her seriousness was evidenced in the astounding picture of gentlemanly propriety before him—tonight was about convincing Little River that no harm had been done to either Rozzy's or Rafe's reputations.

The door of the ballroom opened again, and Rafe's opinion of the most exciting point of the evening already coming and going changed immediately. Rozzy stepped inside, surveying the scene with an irritated pinch of her lips and looking more like the proper Miss Rosaline Pender than he had ever witnessed in his life.

By golly, she was breathtaking too.

"I'd say you're a lucky fellow, Rafe," T.J. said in a low voice, clapping Rafe on the shoulder. The affection he'd felt for T.J.—and he'd hung around the Arrow C enough to call the Nickel family his family too—reflected in the proud smile T.J. gave him, almost like he was Rafe's father and not the father of the stunning bride-to-be. It was one thing to prove himself good enough for Matilda Pender's daughter. It was quite another to have T.J.'s approval. Folks said that Rozzy Pender had the men in her family wrapped around her finger—from Big Ed on down to Bert—but no one doted more on her than this rough-and-tumble cowboy.

Despite the warmth that grew in his belly at T.J.'s approval, Rafe couldn't quite bring himself to call his situation lucky. For as long as he remembered, he'd wanted to marry Rozzy, and to all the town of Little River, it looked as though he might get his wish. And he would have, someday, he felt sure. In due time he could have convinced Rozzy of his genuine feelings, but some blasted puppies and Mrs. Pender's short-sighted matchmaking schemes had turned it all upside down. The only good that had come of the whole thing was Henry Granger backing out of the picture. Rafe could at least be grateful for that.

"Thank you, sir," he managed to choke out. And then he stepped forward to meet Rozzy. It took some courage to reach out and take his "intended's" arm and lean in for a polite kiss on the cheek—just like those highfalutin folks he saw in magazine pictures. Though he would inherit the second-largest ranch in the county and kept company with the Nickels on a regular basis, he'd never considered himself the society type. He'd been raised as Rozzy's social equal by default, not by training. It made what should have been a sweet gesture feel wrong to him. He would have liked to linger over her soft cheek and take a few more breaths of the sweet scent of roses that hung around her.

"Isn't this the most ridiculous spectacle?" she said in an exasperated whisper. "Why—heaven have mercy—is Daddy wearing a tuxedo?"

The tension in Rafe's chest eased up a bit at her shock. A chuckle wormed its way through him. "He is. Spoke to him myself."

"Well, I'll be."

"Rosaline, Mr. Adams . . ." Mrs. Pender made a beeline toward them, her arm snaked tightly through T.J.'s. For the first time in a while, T.J. walked alongside her with a high chin and a confident smile of the man with the prettiest lady in the room next to him. (Well, second prettiest, in Rafe's opinion.) And what's more, he'd stopped tugging at his collar and smiled as though he couldn't be happier to allow Mrs. Pender to lead him around like a prized stallion.

"Oh, so you're Mr. Adams again, even though she believes you to be her future son-in-law," Rozzy said in a wry voice before her parents reached them.

"Oh, my dear." Mrs. Pender's voice had softened, and Rafe didn't miss the way her eyes shone. No doubt Mrs. Pender loved the daughter that exasperated her so, but seeing her all dolled up like a debutante was her dream come true. "You look divine. Oh, T.J, doesn't she?"

T.J. leaned forward and gave his daughter a kiss on the cheek. "She does," he agreed with a proud smile of his own.

Rozzy huffed in response.

Rafe leaned over. "They're right, you know. You're stunning," he whispered, pressing his lips close to her ear. Rozzy might think he played to the handful of guests that had already arrived, but he would enjoy every moment of his engagement to Rozzy. It wasn't going to last long enough anyway. The lucky thing would be if it convinced her to actually marry him, not just say that she would.

She turned, surprise in her expression—he assumed because of his flirting—and arched an eyebrow at him. "You're full of nonsense."

"I am not," he defended himself.

Mrs. Pender, perhaps sensing her daughter's ability to make a scene, broke in. "You two had better follow me and greet our guests. You'll have to see to the ones that have already arrived later." She shuffled Rafe and Rozzy forward, staging them inside the ballroom door as Bert, also dressed to the nines in a smart livery uniform that would rival any grand house in New York, ushered in the Giffords, who owned the Little River First National Bank. They were followed by Tillie and Mrs. Van Doren, which sent a shiver of tension through the entire party at the door.

"How good of you to come." Mrs. Pender bowed her head graciously to Mrs. Van Doren. They shook hands and kissed cheeks, leaving Rafe at a loss as to how *he* should greet the widow of the late town doctor. He settled for shaking her hand and smiling.

"Congratulations, Rafe," Mrs. Van Doren said with a tight-lipped, shrewd smile. It ruined the good looks Mrs. Van Doren had kept, even in middle age. "We had all thought there was to be no engagement, you know."

Beside him, Rozzy squeezed his arm, though when he glanced at her, her cool expression remained in place. "Well, as you see . . ." Rozzy leaned into Rafe. "It must have been a misunderstanding," she said.

Rafe glanced at Tillie, who eyed Rozzy with the same narrow gaze as her mother. "Thank you for your kind words," he said. "I'm quite pleased, Mrs. Van Doren. I've looked forward to this day for quite some time."

"Have you?" Mrs. Van Doren arched her brow. "Well, yes, we all know you've been sweet on Miss Rosaline for some time, but after that business, your attentions seemed to cool."

"As Rosaline said," Mrs. Pender broke in, her thin smile holding more steel than Mrs. Van Doren could ever hope to achieve, "you must have misunderstood."

"Indeed," Mrs. Van Doren replied. "Ah, T.J., how delightful to see you here." The condescending surprise was quite thinly veiled, and everyone within hearing distance understood Mrs. Van Doren's motives. Matilda Pender might rule over Little River society thanks to her wealth and eastern connections, but her eccentric living arrangements with her husband and her lack of control over her daughter made circumstances ripe for a coup.

"Oh, really," Rozzy muttered under her breath. She glared at Bert as he came back with another couple, willing him to save them all.

"Excuse me," he interrupted in his benign tone—the well-bred tone Bert often adopted for Mrs. Pender's parties. "The Wilkinsons have arrived, ma'am."

Mrs. Pender gave Mrs. Van Doren one last icy smile as they gracefully moved away. Tillie whispered loud enough for everyone within fifty feet to hear, "Misunderstanding? Rozzy told me herself they weren't getting married. Mrs. Pender has forced his hand for certain."

Rozzy made a move to follow Tillie, but Rafe held on tight to her arm. "Easy now, Roz," he urged softly.

"That little witch," Rozzy huffed while Mrs. Pender and T.J. turned to welcome the Wilkinsons. "I *told* her I was the one to refuse you, and she said she'd help me make sure people knew that."

"Thought you were smarter than to trust Tillie Van Doren."

"I was desperate."

Something in Rafe's chest twisted. Desperate not to marry him.

Before he could reply, Rozzy went on in a quiet voice. "Mother is going about this the wrong way. We're not supposed to put on a show over our supposed impropriety. It's all supposed to be hasty. She's setting you up for this kind of talk."

Rafe shook away the sting of her words and winked at her, hoping to calm her. She had the heart of a mama bear. If only he could convince her to see him as more than her cub. "I'm not opposed to hastening our match, if you think it will cause less gossip," he teased, and yet he meant every single word. If he got Rozzy to the church quick-like, it might be easier to convince her later of his feelings for her—before she could get away.

"That's not your most terrible idea," she mused. "I could say later that the speed of it all gave me cold feet. You wouldn't come out looking too bad then, would you?"

He rolled his eyes. She couldn't see past her mother's maneuvering, and with every day of this farce passing, he worried about the real state of Rozzy's feelings for him. She had always spoken as though the way people in town assumed they'd end up together amused her, laughing over it with him. Her concern for his ability to marry for love had unnerved him, to say the least. If she could feel so passionately about the possibility of his hopes being ruined, was it possible that Mrs. Pender's plot had ruined Rozzy's hopes? Did she feel more for Henry Granger than she'd ever let on?

He passed through the rest of the congratulations and greetings as best he could, but all the while, he searched his memories for a sign that Rozzy did indeed love Granger. But she'd always spoken of him with the same lightness she gave Rafe's attentions. Or perhaps his devotion to her had been so single-minded, he'd missed the signs.

Once all the expected guests had arrived, Mrs. Pender sent Rafe and Rozzy to mingle side by side. Rafe hadn't been too much involved in the socializing side of life in Little River in the past several years. His mother had died while he was in college, and when he'd returned, he'd only spent enough time with his too-smooth father to focus on running the ranch. Rafe's brothers had forced his father to retire to Cheyenne a year ago, leaving Rafe in charge of the ranch so they could keep an eye on him and keep the Adams name free of any more scandals. He, Beau, and Obadiah would do anything to free them from Wade Adams's less-than-scrupulous means of replenishing the funds to run the Double A that his get-rich-quick (but failed) investments had depleted. Rafe had poured so much effort into keeping the Double A afloat honestly that he'd left his social life behind long ago. Would Mrs. Pender expect him to keep this sort of showcasing up if he married Rozzy?

"Would you like some air, Rozzy?" he asked when they extricated themselves from the Giffords and the reverend and his wife.

"Oh, yes," she said in a sigh of relief.

He took her arm and led her toward the double French doors that opened into the garden. A gray stone path wound to the center of the garden and then broke off into three paths. Cherry blossom trees crowded the end of the path, shading a bench. Colorful bushes and flower beds lined the other paths, and tall Chinese juniper bushes ringed the whole garden. This oasis, such a startling contrast to the brown dust and light-green sagebrush that surrounded the house, was the pride of the town.

Though the sun had set, the air was still warm and heavy with the heat from the day. Rozzy slipped her hand into his, and the friendliness of the gesture broke Rafe's heart.

"Do you do things like this often?" he asked, waving back toward the well-lit house.

"Nothing as grand as that. When the oldest Gifford girl got married this spring, it was quite an event, and Mother insists the Roseboom wedding next month will be quite smashing. She's making me get a new dress, when no one would notice if I wore something I already had." She turned to him with a small smile. "Mother talks and talks about the days when she was in New York. She had a *season*, you know, like the kind you read about in romance novels."

Rafe grinned. "I don't know, actually."

She scowled, but Rozzy had never been able to hold any real anger or frustration in a scowl. Her face was too full of happiness, even with her lips turned into a frown. Without thinking about it, he moved closer so their shoulders touched as they walked. Her presence always brought familiarity and comfort.

"You ought to read one or two. You'd learn ever so much about romance."

He quirked an eyebrow at her. "Are you suggesting I would have done a better job at proposing, then, if I had read one before?"

She drew a breath and then laughed, nudging him with her shoulder The sweet smell of her perfume drifted by him for a brief moment. "Oh, you did such a lovely job. It's too bad you had to waste such pretty words on me."

"None of my words have ever been wasted on you, Roz." He stopped on the stone pathway and turned to face her, taking her other hand in his.

She let her head fall onto his shoulder. "That's such a nice thing to say. Why can't we go on being best friends? I know it might be a little lonely not to ever marry, but we'd have each other, and life has been good, hasn't it?"

Rafe had never been one for dramatics, but the urge to shake her by the shoulders pounded hard against him. My, she had the oddest ideas. "I would like a family, hopefully a son to pass the ranch along to—or a daughter. I'm not picky," he hurried on after she cast him an arch look.

She smiled at his correction but then turned her gaze to the ground. He stood near enough that he saw pink flooding her cheeks. "Of course. I hadn't thought of that."

"And who says we can't be best friends when we get married?" Good heavens, that was one of the biggest reasons Rafe wanted to marry her. He pictured a sort of idyllic life, riding alongside his sweetheart as much as they could, chatting comfortably as they always did. Was that not the sort of thing Rozzy wished for? Was that not romantic enough for her?

"I don't think your wife would like that much—you spending so much time with me."

Rafe pressed his lips together to stop a laugh—though a laugh would be preferable to weeping like a woman over how stubborn this girl was, and thick too. But then, in a quick-passing flicker, he caught teasing in her expression. No—not quite a tease, but a quirk of her lips before she bit down on them. Was she acting thick on purpose?

He took a breath, committing the moment to memory to study later. They had reached the end of the path, coming to a stop under the cherry blossom trees, brightening the whole garden with their pink blooms. He reached to pick one for her, and she brought it to her nose, closing her eyes as she breathed in the sweet sent. Reluctantly, Rafe turned them back toward the party. They couldn't avoid it forever. Mrs. Pender would come looking for them soon, no doubt. He'd seen the way she'd shone tonight, truly in her element. She wouldn't want a moment wasted.

"How did your mother end up married to T.J. if she had an actual *season?*" he asked as they strolled toward the house, Rozzy holding the blossom in one hand, bringing it up to her nose every few seconds.

"Grandfather says she turned down at least half a dozen men head over heels in love with her. Seems none of them measured up in some way. One was too short, another not rich enough." She giggled a bit. "He says she turned down one because his nose was too big." Rozzy paused and stared ahead of them. Through the window, they could see T.J. and Mrs. Pender standing arm in arm and chatting with a couple whose names Rafe couldn't remember, guests of the Nickels for the weekend. They'd ridden the train from Cheyenne for the party. "I think that was about the time Grandfather realized that Mother was gone for T.J. Mrs. Hewitt says that it disappointed Grandmother that she didn't accept a dandy out east, but nobody minded much when she married Daddy."

Rafe cranked his neck to look at the brick mansion before him, smiling to himself. "I suppose Big Ed knows what it means to make his girls happy—and that's all that mattered to him."

Rozzy followed his gaze and nodded. "I believe you're right."

He squeezed her fingers and stared at her. "So what's going to make you happy?" he asked in a soft voice.

Rozzy's gaze didn't move from the house. "To work this ranch until I die."

She'd said it all her life, and Rafe had never begrudged her dream. But he'd hoped that someday he might be the thing that made her happy.

# CHAPTER 8

Rafe's attentive, flirtatious behavior made Rozzy suspicious that he'd taken lessons from her mother in this matchmaking business. Rozzy could only play dumb to his charms for so long before he caught on. He looked so smart tonight in his white waistcoat and tie, his hair combed back away from his face. It hid the tough cowboy beneath, the one who made her stick to a task until she mastered it. Like when he'd helped her practice roping.

As soon as they returned to the party, she made an excuse to get food, waving off his offer to get something for her, and escaped from him for a few moments. Her plan to get out of this wedding grew more complicated every day. Maybe it would have been better to let people talk about Rafe rather than giving him hope for their future. She was selfish, that's what. Hanging on to him and their friendship when it would be better to have the tough talk with him now.

As Rozzy approached the refreshments, she saw Daddy reach for a drink from one of the girls they'd hired to serve. White grape juice with ginger ale and mint, since Mother was quite strict about alcohol, even though the sheriff routinely turned a blind eye.

"Smashing party." Mrs. Van Doren had appeared next to him, reaching for one herself.

Daddy nodded at her with a stiff smile. "I agree." He took a step away, but Mrs. Van Doren laid a hand on his arm.

"You look very dashing, T.J.," she said. With her drink in hand, she sidled right up to his shoulder. Good heavens. One moment the woman was looking down on him for the pretense of their happy family, and the next she was flirting!

"Hello, Daddy," Rozzy interrupted the same time Mother arrived on his other side. Mrs. Van Doren dropped her arm, but the fire in Mother's expression threatened to singe the woman's eyebrows. If Mrs. Van Doren wasn't trying to ruin the party by causing this scene, Rozzy might have enjoyed watching Mother give Mrs. Van Doren a talking-to.

"Matty." Daddy took a long step to distance himself from Mrs. Van Doren's clutches. He nodded at her as Rozzy took his other arm, and the family moved away.

"T.J., how *could* you?" Mother snapped at him. "You promised me—"

"He was only being polite," Rozzy interrupted. It was, perhaps, too much to ask that her parents actually get along as part of the fairy tale they tried to present to the guests. "Mrs. Van Doren practically threw herself at him."

"Rozzy, do not speak to me that way," Mother said, not even turning to look at her daughter, still intent on lecturing Daddy.

Though they were huddled together, Rozzy still caught sight of some guests casting curious looks their way, and Mrs. Van Doren had already recovered enough from her part to stand next to Mrs. Wilkinson with a satisfied smirk.

"Mother," Rozzy said forcefully. "We are about to cause the scene we just escaped." She raised her eyebrows in warning.

Mother stiffened but didn't look around to confirm Rozzy's report. "We'll discuss this later," she said instead.

Rafe, always alert to trouble afoot, arrived at her side. "Miss Rosaline?" That phrase alone melted half the ice in Mother's expression. "Would you like to dance?"

"Of course." Rozzy plastered a lovestruck smile on and took his offered hand, which he then tucked around his arm.

"I suppose that leaves you with Mrs. Pender," Rafe said pointedly to Daddy. He took the hint, pulling Mother along with him.

"Well done, Mr. Adams." Rozzy used his arm to lean closer to him.

"Nothing you didn't have handled." He winked, readjusting his arm to circle it around her waist and then take her hand in his. It struck Rozzy that no other man would know her parents so well or understand how to defuse such a situation. Rafe did it solely for her. He only cared about the whispers of the people in Little River because it bothered Rozzy. He took care of her. Always.

She leaned her cheek against his smooth chin and drew in a deep breath. He didn't smell like the Rafe she knew—clean air mixed with sweat and cows—but she didn't dislike the still-familiar pine scent of his aftershave. "Thank you," she whispered.

"You're welcome," he whispered back.

Daddy was at breakfast when Rozzy came down the next morning. It startled her so much, she stumbled as she came into the breakfast room —the smaller of the two dining rooms in the Nickels' mansion. She couldn't remember the last time she'd seen him there, sitting at the ten-seat, rectangular dining table like he was still part of the family. Even when she was a child and Daddy had lived in the house, he'd left early, gone to work his land long before breakfast.

"Daddy?" she asked, coming into the room and stopping next to his chair.

"Say good morning to our guests, Rosaline," Mother said with a tight-lipped smile and a tip of her head down the table.

Ah yes, now it all made sense. Mother was putting on a show for the guests from Cheyenne and Denver, even though if they knew the family well enough to travel that distance for the engagement party, they surely knew about the family's living situation. Rozzy bit back a sigh and did as she was told. It was nonsensical. In another life, if Mother hadn't been the wealthy rancher's daughter, she would have made a fine actress—always playing a part in the life she had planned. Most everything was already picture perfect for her—the charming house, the pretty cream-colored dishes with a blue thistle pattern, the polished mahogany table. One could step into the Big House and believe they'd stepped right into one of those fancy mansions on the Hudson River in New York.

"Good morning." Rozzy smiled at the two couples sitting farther down the table. Papa Ed knew them through his business, she thought she remembered. She took a step down from the empty chair next to her father, kissing her grandfather on the cheek. "Good morning, Papa."

"Mornin', Miss Rozzy." He patted her shoulder. Mother tensed at the nickname—though Papa Ed was the only person alive that Mother never corrected. "I'd say yesterday evening was a fine success, wouldn't you?"

Rozzy had spun some story about turning Rafe down because she thought he only felt duty bound to marry her but then he had convinced her of his true feelings. This story had won over at least the reverend's wife and a few of her friends. Tillie and Mrs. Van Doren still seemed skeptical, although the romance of it had Bess on the verge of swooning, especially when Rafe had grinned, moon-eyed, at Rozzy all night.

"Yes, Papa. I think so." She moved to go to the sideboard for some toast and eggs, but Papa Ed held her hand, squeezing it in his big, callused one. He was shorter than her father, but just as stocky and barrel chested. And though he'd brought more than enough money when he'd moved from out east, he'd worked this ranch along with his hands for a long time. He still had some of the gentleman he'd been raised as in him, but he was also a cowboy now too. He was exactly what Mother wished Daddy would be.

"You can't do any better than Rafe Adams, darlin', you hear?"

"Yes, of course I know that, Papa," she said in a half-strangled voice. It turned her stomach something fierce to lie about their engagement to appease Mother and to keep the town from gossiping, but to mislead her grandfather made her downright sick. She'd ridden with this man all over this ranch starting from the time she was two years old and on his horse with him. He'd gotten quite the lecture from Mother too when they'd gotten back, but it hadn't stopped him from doing it again. She respected him more than any other person on earth.

"Much better than that city boy you kept talking of hitchin' yourself to. Rafe's a fine man. There's nobody I'd trust more with this ranch than him."

Rozzy scowled, guilt fleeing to make way for indignation. "Except me, Papa," she reminded him. "You're leaving the Arrow C to me, unless you've changed your mind?" It rubbed her like a pair of wet pants that Papa Ed insisted on her marrying in order to inherit the ranch. This was exactly why. He'd expect her husband to do the management. For a man that had raised her between the reins of a horse, he had a heaping lack of trust in her.

"Rosaline," Mother said in a warning tone.

"You know I've always wanted you to marry first. Don't get a twist in your skirt. Rafe is an experienced rancher, and it will be good for you to have him by your side." Papa Ed fixed her with a stern glare, ignoring Mother's hope of turning the conversation.

"You're the heiress of quite a spread, Roz, and not just the Arrow C," Daddy added. "Big Ed is right to be glad to have someone like Rafe to run it for you."

"Really," Mother huffed. "You two act like you didn't intend for her to run your land from the second you put her on a horse."

Rozzy could have cheered to hear her mother champion her cause like that. But of course, she'd argue anything against Daddy. Maybe if Rozzy could get him to talk up how much he wanted this wedding, Mother would change her mind.

"They've given us the right to vote," one of the women down the table said. "Is it such a stretch that we can manage our own land as well?"

Papa Ed scoffed, as did one of the other men, and the other woman gave a polite "hear, hear" to the woman across from her. Just like that, the conversation turned from Rozzy to politics, and she gave a sigh of relief. Papa Ed might be a bit softer on some things than Mother, but she'd gotten her stubborn streak from somewhere, since people all said that Rozzy's grandmother had been the sweetest thing you could imagine. She'd never convince him in a head-to-head argument that she was fit to run this ranch without Rafe or anyone else.

No sooner had she sat down between Daddy and Papa Ed than Bert stepped into the room, still all done up in his livery like the night before.

Poor man. He would have to put his costume on for the guests for who knew how many days. Mother reveled in hosting like this, putting on the show for her Western friends, showing them a real high-society household.

"Mrs. Plummer is here, ma'am," he said to Mother.

"Take her on up to Rozzy's room, and we'll be right up," Mother said. Bert gave a small nod and left.

"Mrs. Plummer? Why is she here? And why to my room?" A sort of fear rose in Rozzy's chest. More new dresses? This three-ring circus was getting worse by the minute.

"Rosaline." Mother laughed lightly. "The wedding is in a month, and Mrs. Plummer will want to get started on the dress right away."

Not just any new dress. *The* dress. A wedding dress. Rozzy sat, staring at her mother for several seconds. A picture of herself walking down the aisle toward Rafe in a lacy dress like she saw in the magazines made something flutter in her stomach before she dismissed it. She had better come up with a solution to this situation on the double before Mother got in too deep. Her enchantment with the party the night before had been a warning sign to Rozzy. Mother missed the sparkle and excitement of the society she remembered in New York, and she would do all she could to milk this engagement for as many events as she could —and who knew what monstrosity she'd make of the wedding if Rozzy allowed it? A wedding she couldn't, in good conscience, ever let happen. Not if she and Rafe wanted to be happy.

She knew well enough to keep her mouth shut at the table, though, and save her arguments for when she was alone with Mother. She hurried through her breakfast as much as she could until Mother shooed her away from the table and out of the breakfast room.

As they approached the stairs, Rozzy said in a low voice, "Mother, I don't need a wedding dress. I can wear one of the many gowns I've worn once to some party."

"Don't be ridiculous," Mother snapped. "You will not wear some regular old party dress on your wedding day!"

"You are making much too big a deal of this, considering the whole point is to marry me off because of my tainted reputation."

"Nonsense. No one believes anything actually occurred in that barn." Mother waved her hand at Rozzy.

Rozzy stopped on the stairs and turned to face her mother. "What in heaven's name am I being bustled off to marry Rafe Adams for, then?"

Mother rubbed at her temples in exasperation. "Rosaline, don't you *want* to marry Rafe?" She continued on up the stairs, expecting Rozzy to follow, which she did.

"It's quite unfair to force him into this spectacle."

"Rafe Adams is a capable young man with a mind of his own. He wouldn't have proposed if he wasn't willing to marry you." Mother paused before they reached the open door of Rozzy's room, where they could hear Mrs. Hewitt's and Mrs. Plummer's voices.

"Everyone is *willing* to do your bidding," Rozzy retorted as she marched past and into the room.

"In this case, Rafe was *exceptionally* willing," Mother replied in the same mocking tone Rozzy had used.

Seemed Rozzy couldn't escape the guilt of this lie. Rafe had spoken awfully sweet to her the day he proposed. She'd tried to convince herself he'd played up the part for Mother's sake, but given her suspicions about his feelings, he'd likely planned on something like this all along. Just with a little less pushing from Mother.

"Because he's a good man," she huffed, the heat of anger battling in her belly to overcome the twisted guilt. This was Mother's fault for putting him up to it in the first place. Rozzy could've talked him down gently over time if not for all the uproar over the puppies.

"Of course he is." Mother's expression went soft, and she waved her hand toward Mrs. Hewitt and Mrs. Plummer, who stood in the room discussing some chiffon fabric. It wouldn't do to discuss the many reasons she couldn't marry Rafe in front of the dressmaker when they had all worked so hard spreading the story that he was madly in love with her—a leap that most people in town had taken without question.

"Well, here she is." Mrs. Plummer came forward with her hands out and her expression dreamy. She grabbed Rozzy's hands in hers and squeezed them, looking on with the aura of a proud mama. Of course, over the years, Rozzy and her mother had patronized Mrs. Plummer's shop so much, she must feel almost a kinship to them. "What do you have in mind, dear?" she asked gently.

Rozzy chewed on her lip. Getting through the engagement party and convincing everyone how in love she was had proved difficult enough, but there seemed no end to the charades she had to play. "Everything has happened so suddenly, I guess I haven't really thought about it."

Mrs. Plummer chuckled, then led Rozzy to the bed, where she'd set out some books. A few lay open, their pages filled with fine dresses of all kinds. "Isn't that like you, Miss Rosaline?" she clucked.

Rozzy bent over one of the books, and her breath caught. She'd never been one for too many frills, but planning a wedding couldn't help but pull out the daydreams from a girl. She reached down to run her fingers over the picture of a girl with a floor-length veil of lace, the top almost a cap on her forehead secured by ribbon with trails down near the model's ear and a large, lavender flower at her temple.

"That's quite pretty," she said in a soft voice. The more logical part of her demanded that she remember that she was *not* marrying Rafe if she could help it . . . but it didn't hurt a girl to have ideas. She would marry someday—Papa Ed expected it—perhaps when she convinced Henry to go against his mother. Or when she found someone else who wouldn't butt into the ranch business and would let her do her own thing. As she slowly turned the pages of the book, looking at one beautiful dress after the next, she found herself wondering if Rafe was also going through the motions of seeing to getting a tuxedo—for Mother would insist that he have a tuxedo. Then she found herself picturing him in his tuxedo, and the vision from before, of her making her way down the aisle to him, claimed a spot in her mind once again.

She paused to consider it this time. Rafe would make an excellent husband. He was her best friend, and she wouldn't mind spending the rest of her life with him, if she was honest. But only if they could go on like they did now, without all the love and emotion to ruin their perfect friendship. Well, and if he wasn't a rancher himself. She remembered Daddy and Papa Ed's talk of how having Rafe at her side would do the ranch a world of good. As if she couldn't do the ranch a world of good all on her own.

She shoved the book off her lap, more determined than ever to fix the mess she'd created. She had to find some way to spare the town talking about Rafe badly. Make them see him in the most sympathetic, good light. She'd gone to all this trouble to keep nosy folks like Tillie Van Doren from speaking ill of him, so it wouldn't do any good to get them all in a fuss again over him.

"Well, what do you think?" Mrs. Plummer asked expectantly. Her brows had drawn down in confusion at the way Rozzy handled the book.

"You and Mother ought to pick something," Rozzy said, plastering on a sweet smile. "You would know what was best anyway." Hadn't they told her that for years in the first place? Picking out all the dresses and this kind of fabric, and oh, won't that compliment her figure so?

"You must have an opinion about something, Rosaline," Mother said in a too-patient tone.

Rozzy stood. "Oh, I hadn't realized that was allowed." She held out her arms in a T-shape, the way she always did when Mrs. Plummer measured her, and waited. After several moments of awkward silence while Mother studied her with narrowed eyes, she waved for Mrs. Plummer to get to work.

# CHAPTER 9

The more Rafe thought about it, the more he decided that Rozzy Pender did indeed know how he felt about her. The question remained, though, why she'd declined his proposal and why she put up such a fuss about marrying him.

The most obvious explanation seemed that she didn't return his affection, but he didn't believe that. They shared a deep, unmistakable friendship. When he'd gone away to college, she'd filled her (quite frequent, if he did say so) letters to him with complaints about missing him and how her lessons with her governess bored her so much she'd fallen asleep three times in one week alone. The letters had lacked romance, of course, but then again, she'd only been fourteen when he'd first gone away. They spent almost every day together, although the proposal had strained things between them recently.

So perhaps Rozzy just didn't recognize that she loved him in return. The truth was, he couldn't accept the fact that she might not love him. Not until he had it proven to him.

He'd hoped that his proposal, hasty and forced as it was, would open her eyes—but she couldn't see beyond saving them both from a marriage forced upon them by her mother. And it was time he set to fixing that, especially before Rozzy took too drastic a measure to put a stop to Mrs. Pender's wedding planning enthusiasm. Something Rozzy had said to him at their engagement party had stuck—her questioning if he'd ever read a romance novel. Of course, he hadn't, but he ought to remedy that. He needed to romance Rozzy and put her in a mind to discover her feelings for him.

He took off his second-best cowboy hat as he entered the town's small library and smoothed a nervous hand over his still-wet hair. He always made sure to clean up when he came into town, and now, more than ever, he needed to maintain his gentleman-rancher status to keep Mrs. Pender happy.

"Why, hello, Mr. Adams." The librarian, Miss Maggie, hurried around her desk, her cheeks pink with a slight blush. Rafe wasn't a stranger to this library. He'd borrowed many a book during his school years, back when Miss Maggie volunteered and helped her aunt, the old librarian. He'd studied hard to get himself into Purdue, and he still read as much as he could to make sure his ranching business did its best.

"I've got a new issue of *The Farm Journal*. I'm sure you'd be inter- ested in." She clasped her hands in front of her deep red dress with a tan floral print on it.

He cleared his throat. "I think I'll browse around a bit." He dipped his head to her and began strolling around the library, taking a leisurely route to the magazines to find one his mother used to read. He glanced over his shoulder to make sure Miss Maggie wasn't watching him—but she was. She fluttered her fingers at him, though her cheeks darkened in color a bit, and then ducked her gaze to the books piled in front of her. All that was now visible was the top of her head and her shining locks of auburn hair.

Shaking his head to himself and feeling heat rise up his own neck, Rafe shuffled in front of the pile of magazines with a couple embracing on the cover and the title *Love Stories* scripted across the top. Well, a fella had to learn about this from somewhere. He picked up a few of the latest copies and made his way back to the desk. If the heat in his face said anything, his cheeks must match the deep scarlet of Miss Maggie's.

He cleared his throat as he set them on the counter. "I thought Miss Rozzy might enjoy these," he said.

"Oh, isn't that so sweet of you." Miss Maggie arched an eyebrow at him before she leaned forward to reach for the magazines. Her short hair fell in front of her face, disguising her expression for a moment, but Rafe bit his tongue to keep from commenting. Even after the glittery engagement party out at Big Ed's, folks still whispered about Rozzy turning Rafe down at first.

"That mother of hers likely turned her ear something fierce," he'd heard Mr. Jacobs, the grocer, saying when he'd stopped in to get a shave earlier. Mr. Wheeler, the barber, had hushed him quick when he'd caught sight of Rafe walking in.

"Did you stop and get her some flowers too?" Miss Maggie asked. "Always softens up a girl's heart, if you ask me."

"Miss Rozzy's heart is plenty soft," he said, keeping the gruff out of his voice over having to explain yet again. His mother's admonition of choosing honey over vinegar to catch flies in made him lean over closer. "If you'd like the truth . . ." he said, his voice a conspiratorial whisper.

Miss Maggie's eyes widened, and she nodded so hard the ends of her hair whipped against her cheeks.

"She thought her mother had talked me into it. Told me how she couldn't bear to marry me if I didn't love her as much as she did me." Well, that was the story they'd told at the party, and it had made a fair share of women sigh. If he could get it to spread around town, Rozzy could forget about defending his honor and focus on falling in love with him.

"Oh!" Miss Maggie put a hand to her heart.

Rafe nodded gravely. "Near broke my heart to hear she didn't know how much I've always loved her. Took a fair bit of convincing, if you know what I mean." He winked, and Miss Maggie stumbled back a step.

"My, that's romantic," she whispered.

Rafe rocked back in relief. Miss Maggie would tell that bit of nonsense all over town. Maybe Rozzy'd listen in a bit. Maybe even *she'd* believe it.

Miss Maggie finished checking out his magazines and watched him leave a few minutes later with a sigh and another finger wave. Two ladies he recognized from town opened the door to the library as he pulled away. He chuckled. Miss Maggie would repeat the story to them right away, and from there it would spread through the ladies in town.

He set the magazines in the seat of the truck, and then embarrassment made him rest his hat on top as he drove back to the ranch.

He put the magazines in his saddlebag that afternoon when he headed out to ride his range. As he leaned over his saddle, watching cows, he pulled one out and began flipping through, scanning the beginnings of the stories and only pausing his study when he came upon the interesting sections—those that involved the hero winning a kiss or time alone with his beloved. He put the words to memory, keen on taking his fiancée for another stroll in the garden this evening when he went to call on her. By the time he rode back to the ranch house several hours later, he had a pleased smile on his lips.

# CHAPTER 10

"You have a phone call, miss," Bert said, bringing Rozzy out of her thoughts as she paused on the porch to pull off her boots. It would irritate Mother like a bur in the saddle that Rozzy had snuck out to inspect some old outbuildings with the ranch foreman, Ray. She wanted the guests to believe that Rozzy's role in the ranch management was as an overseer-in-training, prepared to step into her grandfather's boots without getting her hands too dirty. Sitting atop a horse and watching the men do the work.

She furrowed her brows. "Really? Who is it?" She hoped it wasn't Mrs. Plummer, calling to ask for Rozzy's opinion on some small detail of the dress she and Mother had picked out. Of all the things Rozzy had been called on to do for this fake engagement, feigning interest in a dress she never planned on wearing took the greatest toll on her. She kept daydreaming standing next to Rafe in the church and beginning a life together that looked much like the one she lived now, only with Rafe as a much closer partner. Her cheeks heated. But those were just that—daydreams. Like the way her mother had Daddy staying here at the mansion to pretend for their friends.

"Mr. Granger," Bert said, clearing his throat.

"Oh!" Rozzy hurried inside. She'd called Henry several times over the last few days and been told he was out every single time. She hoped he hadn't gone and started courting some other heiress so soon. Perhaps if he had, he'd recommend a friend for Rozzy's cause.

She picked up the shining black receiver from the cradle. "Hello? Henry?"

"Hello, there, baby," Henry's smooth tone said. She cringed at the pet name but gave a soft laugh anyway. "I've a dozen messages here from you."

"Yes, dear," she said, making her own tone sweet as she readied herself to beg for Henry to take her back. "You know I've been devastated since you called everything off."

"Have you?" Henry chuckled. "Mother says Mrs. Pender has put on quite a spectacle over your engagement to that neighbor of yours."

Drat. Gossip traveled far too fast for Rozzy's liking. "That's all for show, Henry, dear." She put a great deal of pouting in her voice. Enough to make her gag on it. "You know I'd much rather marry someone smart like you and not some old cowboy. Between you and me, we can see all the good that's done my mother." Her skin prickled at the lie. But she was doing this to save Rafe from a lifetime of misery —and her ranch from her grandfather's misguided patriarchy. "There's no better match for either of us," she pointed out, hoping he got her message.

"You know my mother," Henry said, his tone turning serious for the first time. "She's too strict to budge an inch on this, baby."

"Oh, but Henry, promise you'll think about it. Think about me." Rozzy made her voice breathy with hope and fear, taking a glance around her to make sure no one overheard her making an absolute fool of herself.

"I'll try," he said, and the call ended.

Rozzy replaced the receiver, uneasiness scampering through her like one of Queenie's puppies. What would she do if Henry wouldn't reconsider? She frowned and looked down at the silver platter on the telephone table, full of letters all addressed to Mother. Some were from New York and several from Denver, probably filled with congratulations from acquaintances Mother had kept in contact with and visited over the years. Rozzy had gone out east with her mother a time or two, but she preferred staying on the ranch to traveling and the overdone glamour of those big-city societies.

If Rozzy sent Henry a devoted love letter, would it change his mind? He was still her best bet at getting the marriage she wanted and a husband her father and grandfather *couldn't* turn to in order to run the ranch. She needed to get herself to Denver to convince him in person. But with Mother caught up in her wedding to Rafe, she couldn't ask to go see Henry.

To top it off, if she threw Rafe over for someone else, especially for Henry and her original, long-standing engagement, the town would pity him. Wouldn't that be better in the long run? They would view her as the villain, which she could stand if it meant having her ranch her own way. No Rafe to take it over for her, as Papa Ed and Daddy seemed to think best.

It took all Rozzy had not to smirk as she walked into the parlor for afternoon tea. She handed over the letters she'd gathered up to her mother, and since her mother was alone, she jumped right in, even though she hadn't finalized how to accomplish everything yet. That would come.

"Does the wedding have to be in a month?" she asked tentatively, taking a seat next to her mother. "You did say that no one really believes anything improper happened—"

"You *not* marrying Rafe will put the idea right back in their heads," Mother said, scowling up at Rozzy from her chair. She gripped the letters so tightly she crinkled the edges.

"That's not what I mean," Rozzy hurried on. To convince Mother to give up on the marriage, she would have to give her something better— marriage to a real gentleman, to Henry, and the possibility (even if Rozzy never intended it to happen) that her daughter would leave the ranch and live a socialite's life. "I meant that if we delayed the wedding, we might have time to go to Denver to buy the things I need to set up house—and new dresses, of course. I've been looking at some of those magazines . . ." She bit her lip, wondering if her mother would believe any of the words spilling from Rozzy's mouth. She hadn't touched that magazine since Mrs. Plummer's visit. She didn't like the way thoughts of marrying Rafe tugged at her heart every time she so much as thought of that dress. "Anyway, I don't have anything I need, it seems. And really, I can't buy the proper . . . items here in Little River." For the life of her, Rozzy couldn't think of one specific thing. Hopefully Mother would chalk that up to Rozzy spending most of her life caring more about the ranch than anything else.

Mother narrowed her eyes but then took a deep breath. "You don't like Denver," she said, but the layer of hope to her words told Rozzy her idea was working.

"But for a wedding . . ." she said, reaching to pour the tea. "That will only happen once, and is there really any other place to buy . . . those sorts of things? Other than maybe New York," she mused, but then she hurriedly added before her mother got too-grand ideas, "but New York is too far. We wouldn't want to put the wedding off *too* long."

"Yes." Mother used one of the letters to fan her face as she studied Rozzy, her eyes brightening with every second. "I know Cecily would love to have us," she said of one of her friends in Denver. They'd remained close through their letters over the years, and Mother always stayed there when she visited. "We wouldn't have to delay the date too long, and we haven't had anything printed yet."

"Oh, Mother!" Rozzy set down her teacup and clapped her hands. The delight surprised her mother, but she recovered in the blink of an eye, a grin spreading across her face as she laid down the letters on the small table next to her. Mother and her friends would insist on parties and dinners, and Rozzy was bound to find Henry at one of them. The Grangers socialized in the same circles—that's how they'd come to their understanding in the first place.

"I'll have Bert send a telegram to Cecily right away. I knew you'd catch the spirit of this sooner or later." Mother beamed and stood, leaning down to kiss Rozzy on top of the head before she flew from the room. "Bert!"

"Now where is she off to?" Rozzy turned to see that Rafe now stood in the doorway, half turned to watch Mother hurry down the hallway calling Bert's name with increasing impatience.

"To send a telegram. Why, Rafe, you're wearing a dinner jacket." Rozzy tilted her head at him, puzzled. And it wasn't just the jacket, but the shirt and the bow tie—like Papa Ed and Daddy and all the men had worn every night while the guests were here. She didn't know Rafe *had* a dinner jacket, and something jumped in her stomach, not unwelcome, to see him look the part of a gentleman. It was as though he had banished the rancher in him for the evening, no trace of the roughness of the range. He'd combed his hair back, and as he came toward her, his grin grew wider and wider. That dimple of his deepened, and Rozzy's heart rate sped. As she opened her mouth to speak, she found she'd been holding her breath and had to draw a long one in to give air to her words.

But Rafe beat her to it. "Good evening, darling."

Hearing him speak so lovingly—and he did speak lovingly, the words pouring from his tongue like honey on a summer day—caught whatever she had meant to say in her throat as warmth spread in her chest. The dangerous warmth made her let loose a giggle at what must be more of his play acting, but as she looked around the room, she found them still alone. Her giggle turned breathless. "Darling?" she repeated in a hoarse voice. She longed to yank on the reins of whatever was happening here and put a stop to the stampede of feelings rushing through her. But something about Rafe's walking closer and closer made her helpless to do anything.

He reached over and took her hand in his, and their roughness brought back the reality that this *was* her Rafe—dressed up and so handsome, but her Rafe—caressing the back of her hand with his thumb. Then he raised it to his mouth and kissed her palm.

Rozzy Pender had never been the fainting type. She had helped her father pull a calf or two, seen the mess it made, and gritted her teeth and carried on. Yet the brush of Rafe's lips—so soft, such a startling contradiction to the familiar coarseness of his hands—sent a full shiver through her, and she began to feel very lightheaded indeed.

"Rafe," she said in a stern voice, attempting to settle her senses. But her heart beat swifter than Irene at a quick trot. This was the exact sort of thing that had gotten her mother into trouble. "There's no need to act like that. We're the only ones in the room."

He shrugged. "Who knows who may step in?" He still held her hand, and he used it to draw her closer, circling her waist with his other arm and pressing his hand into the small of her back. "Will you greet your fiancé with a kiss, dear?"

Rozzy let out a little gasp of surprise, and her heart sped to a full-blown gallop. "I'm not sure that's quite proper," she sputtered, but even though she should pull away and put a stop to this, she didn't. This was different from the lovestruck way Rafe had acted at the engagement party.

"I read one of those romance stories, like you suggested." Since he held her so close, Rafe had lowered his voice to a husky whisper that sent Rozzy's mind spinning. Her knees wobbled, and she might have toppled over like a newborn calf if Rafe hadn't been holding her. "And all the heroes are granted kisses by their beloveds."

This moment had played out like one of those silly stories Rozzy read, but it felt much more than silly. It thrilled her to hear Rafe speak in those soft, loving tones, to have him hold her so near, to really look into the pale blue eyes she thought she knew. To think she might see more than the usual adoration there—to see so much more. And to want it too.

"Well," she found herself saying in a soft voice of her own, "if you think you must." She closed her eyes and waited to see what her first kiss would hold. After all, granting that right to Rafe seemed the least she could do after she'd made a muck of their engagement. And she was prepared to be quite generous to make up for it.

"Rosaline! *Really*." Mother's voice broke the moment, and Rozzy's eyes fluttered open.

Rafe raised his eyebrows but managed to wrangle that devilish smile into contrition when he turned to Mother and slid his hand from Rozzy's waist. "Forgive me, Mrs. Pender," he said, and he tipped his head to Mrs. Collins, one of the guests who must have come down for dinner.

"I'm not completely hardhearted, Rafe, but you ought to choose more out-of-the-way places to steal your kisses," Mother chided, not quite holding back a smile of her own. Rozzy blushed to think of her mother saying such things, but of course she'd like nothing better than to see that even though she'd forced Rafe and Rozzy together, they were in love after all.

Mrs. Collins winked at them, gave a little sigh, and shared a oh-to-be-young look with Mother.

"My goodness, Rosaline," Mother went on. "What are you wearing? Go change for dinner."

Rozzy pressed a hand over her still wildly thumping heart and thought with fright about how badly she had wanted to kiss Rafe. Badly enough that she'd forgotten how dirty she was, that she wore only socks on her feet. She scampered away, glancing over her shoulder at Rafe and worrying over the thread that drew her back to him. She had better get to Denver and convince Henry to take her back. She needed a less dangerous option as soon as possible.

# CHAPTER 11

Rafe whistled as he milked his cow, Daisy. He didn't usually bother with the chore—it was one that he left for the ten-year-old son of his housekeeper. He paid Mrs. Cowles's boys to do some of the farm chores he didn't have time for and didn't want to waste his hands' time on. But this morning he'd woken up with the same grin he'd gone to bed with and thought he'd give Samuel a break for the morning. He'd wake the boy up when he went back to the house for breakfast.

"What are you doing in here, boss?" Jim strode in and eyed Rafe with a cocked eyebrow.

"Milking a cow," Rafe replied, and he went on whistling.

Jim leaned against the cow's stall, amusement in his expression. "What's that tune you're whistling?"

Rafe shrugged. "Something from the radio that Mrs. Pender played last night, I'm sure." More than sure. He'd asked Rozzy to dance to it. The rest of the dinner guests had followed their example, but Rafe had danced in his own world with Rozzy in his arms. Frequenting the town dances as often as he could over the years in order to see Rozzy, to hold her, and to flirt with her had made him an excellent dancer, and they had moved around the parlor floor at a gentle sway with easy steps.

Rozzy had leaned her head against his, her soft curls brushing his cheek. He grinned and kept on whistling.

"You haven't been in a mood like this since before Miss Rozzy turned down yer first proposal." Jim pushed his hat back on his head and let loose a full-toothed grin.

"I believe I may be on the path to winning Miss Rozzy's heart once and for all, Jim." Rafe tipped back on his stool, his good mood still winging around him. He had acted the attentive suitor all night, much as he had the night of the engagement party but more personally. Whenever he had called her "darling" with real feeling, her fingers would flutter in front of her heart, and she would look away with pink in her cheeks. And the expectation in her expression—eyes closed and all—when he'd nearly kissed her? Well, his own expectation burned through his chest. Mrs. Pender had said he was welcome at every dinner at the ranch house while they entertained, and he meant not to miss a one. Before many more nights passed, he hoped to steal that kiss—it would be a wonder if Rozzy went on with this nonsense about getting out of the wedding then.

"That's a good thing, boss, seeing as how you intend to marry her." Jim chuckled, probably at what Rozzy called Rafe's moon-eyed expression.

"I do intend to marry her—and to convince her I'm not doing so just to please her mother." Rafe stood and lifted the milk bucket so Daisy wouldn't kick it over. "I've got some real courtin' to do to convince her I'm serious about marrying her. Doesn't seem to matter what I say—she thinks I'm only going along with Mrs. Pender, and she's determined to save me from my doom."

"And is this where you got such sage advice from?" Jim pulled a rolled-up magazine from his back pocket and held it open toward Rafe.

Rafe colored at the sight of the romantic magazine he'd read on the trail—and likely left in his saddlebag—but strode toward Jim to take it as though it didn't bother him a bit. "And where else is a fella supposed ta get advice on things like that with his mother in the grave? You?" He nodded his head back toward the cow, taking on his boss voice. "Take care of Daisy, will ya?"

"Yes, boss." But Jim chuckled behind Rafe's retreating back.

He rolled his eyes to himself and shoved the magazine into his own pocket. He might have to buy Miss Phelps a new one for the library, what with the wear this copy was getting. Careful not to slosh the milk around as he brought it into the kitchen, he let some words roll around in his head. A poem would be just the kind of romantic thing that would turn a girl's head.

IF ANY OF his men caught him hunched over his saddle, scribbling on a notebook, Rafe would sure get a ribbing. None of his boss-man ordering around would save him face then. But convincing Rozzy of his true affection was more important than anything, even the ranch, these days. He carefully copied out the lines he'd already written on to a new paper to give to Rozzy. He hoped to read it to her, but perhaps she'd like to read it afterwards and think of the moment she'd realized she loved him in return.

Thudding hooves brought his attention up, and he slammed the book shut and shoved it into his saddlebag, making a mental note to be sure he took it out when he got back to the house. Having Jim find the magazine was one thing; having him find the many pages of scribbles as he struggled to write something worthy of Rozzy would give his foreman far more cause for teasing than necessary. She was the only one who ever thought anything of his attempts at poetry.

When he looked up, though, it wasn't one of his men riding toward him but the girl herself. Her hair was pinned back in elaborate twists, like it had been every day he'd seen her the last week or so, but stray hairs flew around her face as she charged toward him. She slowed as she reached him, and he slid off his horse to greet her, grateful that she did the same.

He took both her hands in his. "Hello, sweetheart," he said, careful to use a term of endearment as the heroes of the stories he'd read in the magazine always did.

"Oh, stop it. There's no one out here for miles," she said, yanking her hands away, but Rafe didn't let it bother him. Her cheeks had turned pink, and he had her flustered.

He slid a finger under her chin and tilted her head toward him, leaning in to brush a soft kiss on her cheek. He worried for a second that she stood close enough to hear his heart hammering at his boldness, at the temptation to slide a few inches to the left and kiss her lips right then and there. "I'm meant to marry you, Roz—my love. Shouldn't I call you sweet things?" He drew back to register her reaction to his latest flirtations.

She stared at him, looking as moon-eyed as she teased him about, and then blinked and looked at the ground. She took a step back, taking her hands away. "That's just it—I've come to tell you I found a way out of this mess. You're saved."

Rafe's heart stopped hammering immediately. "What do you mean?"

"I've convinced Mother that I must buy my wedding things in Denver, and she's taking me there. Today, actually! On the train. Only while I'm there, I'll convince Henry to take me back."

Silence settled between them for a long moment, and for the life of him, Rafe didn't know what to say. He studied her face, looking for any sign of heartache he'd missed in the days since Granger had called off their understanding, but he saw nothing other than embarrassment and the skittishness of an unbroken colt.

"You didn't say anything about it last night? You might have mentioned you planned on leaving." He cursed the way his voice cracked.

"Oh, well, I was going to, and then . . ." She faltered, and when he met her eyes for the brief second that she allowed, he wondered if his attentions to her might have distracted her from mentioning it. Their almost kiss in the parlor had distracted *his* thoughts much of the evening. "You see, Mother's in a hurry so that we don't have to delay the wedding too long, and she telephoned her friend, Mrs. Allred, who said that of course she would have us, and so we're all set to go. Rafe?"

He blinked at her and looked up.

"Rafe, you don't seem happy at all," she said in a timid voice.

"Well, of course I'm not," he cried.

"Oh, now, don't be angry. People will be so busy talking about me marrying Henry in a rush, they'll hardly worry about you. They won't pity you too much, and even if they did, isn't that better than letting Mother force you to marry me?"

In a rush? What did she mean to get herself into? But then he caught it. The innocence in her expression was contrived. She'd used this expression too many times on her mother or Big Ed when they'd gotten in trouble when they were younger. The time they'd ridden one of the new colts and Rozzy had broken her arm, she'd blinked up at Big Ed with these exact wide eyes, framed in long, dark lashes, and convinced him she'd thought it was a different horse until it was too late. Never mind that Rafe had already survived six seconds on that bucking bronc and that she herself had made five before it'd thrown her. Too late indeed.

Before he pointed it out—asked her what it was all about pretending she didn't know about him loving her—she grabbed his hands, her expression desperate for him to understand. He shook them off, though, and turned toward his horse, resting his face against the hindquarters. "I'm only thinking of you, Rafe. Don't you see?"

After a few deep breaths, he spun toward her. "I don't see. You can't be thinking of me, because if you were, you'd see that you marrying Henry Granger is the last thing I want. And the last thing on my mind is how this town is going to talk about me if you jilt me." Desperation of his own coursed through his veins. He'd thought all his sweet talk had made a difference last night, had shown her the path to his true feelings —but all along she'd known that path was there and avoided it.

She twisted her fingers together, not meeting his gaze. "I don't understand." Her voice came out small and frightened.

"Oh yes, you do," he shot back at her. Hurt made his words sharp and as hot as a branding iron. "How long have you known that I love you, Roz?"

Genuine surprise dropped over her expression. "Love?" she repeated. "Why, I knew you were sweet on me, everyone said so, and you've always been so attentive . . . but . . ."

He closed his eyes. "But you pretended not even to know that."

"I thought you, of all people, would understand." Her voice trembled like pine trees in a stiff wind, and it cut through Rafe's heart.

But still the pain rose through him, for the first time stopping him from moving to comfort her. "Understand what?" How long had he made himself for a fool for her while she mocked him with her fake innocence? "Why in the world would you let me kneel in front of you and beg you to be my wife and pretend not to know how I felt?"

She pulled her trembling lips between her teeth, chewing on them before she spoke. "My mother forced you to say such things," she whispered.

"Maybe Mrs. Pender forced me into *when* to propose to you, Rozzy— love, darling, sweetheart—but it was *me* who decided long ago to marry you." He moved one of his hands to cup her cheek and draw her face up to his, and he stole his kiss. And for the first time in this upside-down courtship, it happened in the exact right place: out on the Wyoming range where he had grown to love her in the first place.

Her lips melted into his as he put his other arm around her waist and pulled her to him. Her hands pressed against his shirt and then gripped it, her touch sending jolts of electricity through him as she returned his kiss movement for movement. Hope stampeded through him.

"No. Stop it," she suddenly whispered, pushing away from him. "Stop it! Stop it!" Her voice rose, and she took several steps back. "I can't marry you!"

Nothing Rozzy had ever said struck him the way those words did. Not once in the many times she'd denied before that moment, in some way or another, the feelings she had for him. She'd shared that kiss with him, fallen as deep in as he did, returned his love in the press of her lips to his. Her words made him stumble back into his horse.

She whirled back to him, her expression full of desperation and pain. "If I marry you, I'll never run the Arrow C. Daddy and Papa Ed will let you take it all, even if they say they're passing it on to me. It's what they want."

Rafe let his shoulders slump in defeat. So he hadn't needed to convince her of how he felt or how she felt. She'd known all along, but the ranch was too important. It struck a nerve, reminded him of the way his father would insist that his gambling, his foolish investments, his con schemes were to keep the ranch in Adams hands for his boys. As if he hadn't already lost the fortune he claimed to protect. It had taken years of hard work from all three brothers to get the ranch out of debt and making money again. It had taken seeing his father's excuses as just that—vices he couldn't get the better of.

That's all Rozzy had handed him. An excuse for her fear.

"You don't know me at all." He climbed slowly up into the saddle, staring out across the range instead of at her.

"How can you say that? I've known you all my life," she said, her voice breaking.

"I thought so too." He swallowed hard and looked down at her. "But if you did, you'd know better than to think I'd ever take the Arrow C from you. I'm not my father."

She took a shuddering breath but turned away.

"Looks like we found a way out of this mess, as you like to call it," Rafe went on. "I'll make sure everyone in town knows I'm the one that refused to marry you. Don't you worry about it."

He spurred his horse on and heard her cry from behind him, "You wouldn't dare!" Another time it would've brought a smile to his face, but his heart was too broken for anything like that.

# CHAPTER 12

R ozzy boarded the train that morning, still in a daze from the events that preceded it. It was useless to go to Denver now, with Rafe talking like he would break off their pretend engagement, but she didn't have the courage to say a word of what had happened to Mother. Why, if she knew that Rafe had all but said he really loved her—not because Mother told him to love her—she'd never let Rozzy hear the end of it.

She turned to the train window and pressed a hand over her eyes, forcing back tears and emotion for the hundredth time since Rafe had ridden off. Of all things, it seemed likely she loved that cowboy back. More than she ever suspected. Which meant that marrying him would turn out even worse than she'd thought. She hiccupped a little, unable to keep that bubble of emotion back.

She didn't have much to judge kissing by—well, truth be told, she had nothing to judge kissing by—and still she was quite certain there would never be a thing like the way she had flown while kissing Rafe. She had felt a hint of the softness of his lips on her hand from the night before, and then again when he'd kissed her on the cheek in greeting, but oh, how gently his lips moved over hers in such a careful, thoughtful way so like Rafe. The way he'd put his hand to the small of her back sent fire racing through her. The whole experience still tingled over her skin, more delicious and exciting than anything she had ever known—better even than racing across the Arrow C on the back of her horse and knowing that she belonged to that land.

That's what frightened her so. The notion that maybe she belonged more to Rafe Adams than to the piece of earth she'd thought was her whole being. That he had more power to make her miserable than the thought of losing the ranch forever. They'd end up worse than Daddy and Mother.

Why did he have to go and prove that with his stupid kissing?

She could have gone on in ignorance of how deep her feelings ran for him. She wouldn't have missed out on *too* much not marrying him. But the thought of losing him now churned in her stomach with ferocity. Maybe Mother hadn't turned down half a dozen dandies because she'd found one thing or another wrong with them. Maybe it had happened because loving Daddy had stolen her power to do anything else.

Rozzy was so tangled up she didn't even notice Daddy sitting down across from her until he asked, "What's wrong, little miss?"

She snapped her head up, not sure what to be more surprised by: the fact that the train was moving and he sat across from her, or that he wore a smart traveling suit. "Good heavens, what are you doing here, Daddy?"

He chuckled and arched an eyebrow at her. "I rode all the way into town with you and boarded the train and you're only now noticing me?"

She bit her cheek and shrugged in embarrassment, unwilling to explain what had occupied her mind so. He would hoot and tease when he discovered Rafe had bamboozled her with a kiss.

"I can't let my girls travel all the way to Denver by themselves." He winked at Mother and cast her a charming smile.

The way Mother's eyes twinkled struck Rozzy with surprise, but Mother went on in her usual tone, "Nonsense. It's 1924. We hardly need a chaperone. I've gone to Denver plenty of times without you."

"But you hate Denver—or any city," Rozzy pointed out, still confused over the circumstance.

Daddy gave her a shrewd look. "So do you."

So Rozzy clamped her mouth shut.

BY THE TIME Mrs. Allred's car dropped them at her Capitol Hill home, Rozzy would have died for a long horse ride across an empty stretch of land with nothing but her thoughts for company. But there were no horses, empty stretches, or silences to speak of on the busy street. How did one keep from losing one's mind with the constant roar of motor engines outside?

"Oh my, Rosaline," Mrs. Allred cried when she greeted Rozzy with a kiss to her cheek. "You have quite grown up since the last time I clapped eyes on you. Why, I believe you couldn't have been more than fourteen. Are you sure you want to marry that farmer?" she added with a mischievous smile as she hooked her arm through Rozzy's and moved to the stairs. "I'm sure I know so many smarter—and richer—gentlemen here who would be happy to take you off your mother's hands and put you up in style."

Rozzy tittered, nerves making the laugh sound shrill. She *couldn't* marry that farmer, but a part of her, increasing by the hour, was quite afraid he didn't want to marry her anymore, and that really alarmed her.

Mrs. Allred cast a look back at Mother and Daddy, and her grin widened as she lowered her voice to a stage whisper and said in a dramatically confiding tone, "Don't you worry, dear. We'll send you out in style, and I'll make sure you have plenty of men to flirt with in the meantime." She winked.

Mother laughed from behind them, where she leaned quite heavily on Daddy's arm. "Oh, if only I thought that would tempt her," Mother said.

"Here now," Daddy said. "Rafe Adams is the best of fellows, and someone must defend him."

"We both know I'd never allow my daughter to marry him if he wasn't," Mother shot back in a defensive and haughty tone.

"Let me show you upstairs to your rooms. I'm sure everyone could use a rest before dinner. It's turned into something of an event, Matty. I hope you don't mind. Once word got out that you were coming to town, everyone rang up for an invitation." Mrs. Allred mounted the first step of the marble staircase.

"I certainly don't mind," Mother said. "But does your cook?" The women laughed together.

"Mrs. Allred, I would much rather go for a long walk," Rozzy said. She needed to stretch her legs something fierce after being cramped so long in a train.

"Me too," Daddy said. "I'll see your mother upstairs and accompany you."

Rozzy bit her tongue, ready to protest her need of a chaperone. The antsy look in her father's eyes said he needed the movement as much as she. He'd spent so much time entertaining guests the last few days instead of sitting in the saddle, it was a wonder he'd gotten it into his head to come at all.

Rozzy let Mrs. Allred lead her to her room, where she changed from her traveling clothes into something more suited for walking out in the warm summer weather. Her father met her downstairs, and they headed out on to the street lined with its majestic houses. The styles were so varied that Rozzy found herself admiring them, several colonial-looking ones as well as some of other distinctive styles. Distracting herself with the interesting shapes and details engrossed her so much that neither of them spoke for some time.

"You going to tell me what's eatin' at you, Roz?" Daddy asked after several minutes had passed.

"Oh, I'm tired is all, Daddy. So many parties since this whole thing started, and now this trip. It's enough to wear a girl out." She waved away his concern and avoided his gaze, staring at the street instead and wondering what Rafe was doing.

"This from the girl who once stood up with me all night with that jersey who had a breech calf and got up the next morning for church as though she'd had a full night's sleep? My girl's no wilting socialite."

When she turned back to him, he arched an eyebrow at her. "It's not that unusual for a girl to be distracted with her wedding coming up, is it? Why, you've no idea how many things there are to think of."

"And your mother has every single one of them covered and scheduled down to the minute. I know because she spent half the trip wondering how a girl could be so *disinterested* in the planning—that you told her and Mrs. Plummer to choose the gown because they would know best," he kept on prodding.

Rozzy pressed her lips together, wishing he'd drop the subject but knowing better. A man who'd been married to Matty Pender for so many years wasn't likely to give up too quickly on anything. The fact that he walked along this street with her said a lot—that after ten years of separation, he still hadn't given up on Mother.

"You want to marry Rafe, don't you?" he asked.

It made Rozzy look up. He said it so differently than Mother had over the past few days. She had exasperation and disbelief in her tone. Daddy sounded curious and gentle. "I . . . yes. Of course." That wasn't a lie. Her heart still raced every time she thought of the way his lips felt on hers, and that had her sure she'd never be kissed again the way he had kissed her. She didn't add that she couldn't marry him. Golly, Rafe had made such a mess of things. And that nonsense about her thinking he acted anything like his father? Rozzy wasn't worried about her ranch being conned away from her. Her own father and grandfather had that all covered. They planned on handing it to Rafe without a lick of trouble on his part.

Daddy studied her before turning to nod at a couple of ladies passing by. "Always figured you'd marry Rafe, you know. Always wanted it, to be honest."

Rozzy bristled as she remembered the way he and Papa Ed had celebrated Rafe saving the ranch from her supposedly inexperienced clutches. Of course they wanted her to marry Rafe. They had set it up as earnestly as Mother. In their minds, no one could run the Arrow C better except themselves. She kept her tone calm. Daddy had little to do with what Papa Ed did with the ranch—by his own choice many years ago. "You never said so before my engagement."

"Because you would have dug your heels in and run out here and married the first rich gentleman your mother introduced you to." He chuckled to himself.

"I would not have . . ." Her protest faltered. She planned on something very much like that. How did they expect any different? The only way she'd get to control her ranch was if she married some fellow who hadn't the slightest idea what to do with a decent spread and five hundred head of cattle. Daddy and Papa Ed would *have* to accept her as the one to run the Arrow C. Because even if Rafe would never try to take the ranch from her, her grandfather and father would as good as turn the reins over to him without a second thought the minute she said *I do.*

"That boy's been sweet on you since he first saw you in the cradle, you know?" Daddy's voice had turned gentle and thoughtful, and he pulled Rozzy closer to him. "Picked you right up and held you near an hour, and you making eyes at him the whole time."

Tears stung her eyes, and she had to turn away to hide them. "I've heard that story a hundred times, Daddy."

He stopped their progress up the street and turned her to face him. She had blinked most the tears away, so she tipped her head enough to look him in the eye from under the tilted brim of her felt cloche. "Why did Matty have to force you to accept him when you've loved him just as long?" he asked in a low voice.

She ground her teeth as she tried to find an excuse. "Well, it's like you said. The minute Mother made me do it . . ." She shrugged, hoping he'd lay off all these questions. He was worse than Mother.

"Come on now, Roz. Maybe I haven't lived in the same house for a while now, but I'm clever enough still. You cried for weeks when that boy went off to college without you."

"I was fourteen!" She whirled and stalked back toward Mrs. Allred's house. Perhaps she needed that rest after all. Every question squeezed inside her heart, reminding her how irreplaceable Rafe was. Riding fence lines and pushing cattle would be lonely without him. Every step reminded her that her love for the Arrow C was woven through with love for Rafe too.

Daddy hurried to catch up, grabbing her elbow. "I've only ever seen you really down when you've quarreled with him, little miss." He pulled her to a stop again and added in a gentle voice that made everything inside Rozzy's chest tighten, "What did you quarrel over?"

Her chin trembled, and she turned to the sidewalk as tears gathered in her eyes. "Don't tell Mother, please. If I convince Henry to take me back—or find some other eligible gentleman—she won't mind so much when she finds out Rafe and I have broken things off."

Daddy scowled. "What's this?"

Rozzy squared her shoulders. "You are wrong, Daddy. Rafe doesn't want to marry me—at least not anymore. And I'd be better off with some dandy anyway." She hurried forward, away from his questions and the pain it struck through her to admit the truth. Knowing that Rafe was sweet on her was more important than she'd realized. Even a hundred thousand acres of the Arrow C couldn't fill the empty space rolling through her.

# CHAPTER 13

When Rafe banged into his kitchen late the next morning, he found Jim there eating biscuits and sweet-talking Rafe's widowed housekeeper, Mrs. Cowles. "Thought I told you to move the herd over to Crooked Creek this morning," he snapped at his foreman.

Mrs. Cowles jumped at his frigid tone, but Jim stood and eyed his boss warily. "Can't a man have his breakfast first?"

"Breakfast was hours ago. I don't pay you to flirt with my housekeeper." Rafe put his hands on his hips and glared at Jim. He didn't know if he could stand witnessing his foreman saying sweet things to Mrs. Cowles. More to the point, he didn't know if he could stand Mrs. Cowles accepting his attentions with sweet words of her own.

"Has Miss Rozzy said when she's coming back?" Jim asked pointedly, shoving his cowboy hat back onto his head and slipping another biscuit from the pan on the stove.

Anger seared through Rafe's chest, along with a healthy slice of pain. He wouldn't forget for a long time the way she'd cried that she couldn't marry him—no matter how desperate she'd sounded for him to understand what he never would. He'd never had a lick of interest in running the Arrow C for her. No interest in trying to take something from her. The idea that she'd believed him to be the same as his father! How could she think of him that way when he'd spent a good portion of his life teaching her how to run her own ranch? When she herself had heard him rail on his father's slick ways?

"When Miss Pender returns is no concern of mine," he barked. "What is my concern is whether it was a good idea to keep you on when I took over the ranch, seeing as how you have a difficult time understanding who runs the Double A."

Jim leaned back, startled at Rafe's outburst. "Boss?"

"Move the herd." Rafe's boots slapped against the linoleum floor as he stalked across the kitchen and toward the office that adjoined it. He didn't turn when Jim offered a crisp "yes, boss" and the kitchen door shut with a soft thud.

Rafe sat down at his desk, removed his hat, and tossed it on top. He had some visits to attend to, but he had better let his temper calm first. Jim hadn't deserved the dressing down Rafe had handed him. In reality, Jim respected Rafe more than he'd ever respected his father, which came from the fact that Jim had spent much of his career doing business behind his former boss's back in order to keep things afloat. Rafe and his brothers were grateful for Jim's hard work, but his employees teasing him like he was still a teenager needed to change.

Rafe leaned back in his chair and closed his eyes, wishing that his early-morning responsibilities had taken more of his mind off his argument with Rozzy. Over the years, especially when he'd become serious about courting her, he'd always expected the matter of marrying her to hinge on *when* he would convince her of his feelings, not *if*. His brain had a difficult time accepting the change in circumstance. He had dreamed the night before of riding the range with her and woke longing for her to come home, only to remember that when she did, she would likely be engaged to Granger again with a wedding date set. Possibly the same wedding date Mrs. Pender had set for Rafe to marry her daughter.

He leaned forward and searched through the ledgers on his desk for the one he wished to update after his inspection of one of his herds that morning. He moved aside notes he had received from various matrons of Little River inviting him to a multitude of functions. Since playing the gentleman at the engagement party and other events Mrs. Pender had seen fit for him to attend, his invitations had picked up again. His family had always been a regular part of Little River society, but since the death of his mother and his father's move to Cheyenne, Rafe hadn't socialized as much as they had.

He picked up one from the Van Dorens inviting him for dinner that evening. It might be something to get his mind off what Rozzy was up to and a good start to spreading the word that his and Rozzy's wedding was off. He grabbed up the note and headed back to the kitchen to phone Mrs. Van Doren. He had to get out of this darned house anyway.

# CHAPTER 14

Rozzy set out the next morning to see Henry. She had to have her engagement to him back in place before Mother heard from Little River that Rafe had called things off. Mother would still lecture about the scandal such a reversal would cause, but Rozzy had several ideas for mitigating the whole thing. Like getting married in Denver and throwing a big, highfalutin party that Mother would love.

The Grangers' housekeeper's eyebrows jumped to her hairline when she opened the door to see Rozzy. "Why, Miss Pender. How good to see you. Come in." She held open the door and swept out a hand toward the nearby parlor. "Shall I get Mrs. Granger?"

Rozzy held back a shudder. Perhaps she might need to turn her charms on the matron, but she would rather take a crack at Henry first. "Is Henry in?" she asked, crossing her fingers behind her back.

The housekeeper bobbed her head. "Yes, miss." She led Rozzy to the parlor and then disappeared in search of the gentleman. Henry's preference for working as little as possible at the offices for his father's department store chain had been what attracted Rozzy to him in the first place, and that saved her today from having to go downtown in search of him. She blessed him for it.

"Well, baby," Henry drawled when he strode into the parlor. "This is quite a surprise."

She hurried over to him, taking his hands and leaning up to kiss his cheek, silky smooth from likely just shaving. The scent of his aftershave lingered strong enough to attest to that as well. She forced herself to linger over the touch and not cringe away from how Henry gripped her hands when she leaned into him. "Is it a surprise?" she asked, using the innocence that had irritated Rafe the day before. "What else is a girl to do when her beau won't return calls and refuses to listen to reason?"

"Your beau?" He chuckled and put her arm through his, leading her over to one of the sofas, an ornate thing that must have been a stubborn holdover from Mrs. Granger's youth. "I was under the impression that you replaced me rather swiftly."

Rozzy pouted, scooting closer to Henry. "You know my mother did that only because you threw me over." She called on the desperation that had made her toss and turn most of the night, using it to wheedle Henry to her side of things. "All this over some puppies, Henry? I can assure you that absolutely nothing happened. Must we be so old-fashioned?"

He scrutinized her, his expression pinched with confusion—Henry was always hard-pressed to put much effort into anything. "I guess I didn't realize how much you cared." He ended this statement with a quirk of his brow.

"Of course I care about you!" She leaned forward, pressing her lips to Henry's and forcing herself to find the emotion that had churned inside her when she'd kissed Rafe, something to convince Henry to see things her way. Though the way he put an arm behind her shoulders was gentle, she spent the better part of the kiss convincing her body not to revolt and jerk away.

Henry sighed when he released her, his smile still tilted with confusion. "Do you plan to use that argument to convince my mother?" he asked as he drew away.

Rozzy forced a laugh. "Well, Henry," she said, ignoring the heat in her cheeks from the embarrassment of using the kiss to get to him. "I can certainly promise that a life with me is a much more satisfying prospect than one with your mother." She kept her smile light and expression teasing, but Henry flinched, assuring Rozzy that he took her meaning.

"Yes," he murmured, still staring at her, his own smile forced. "I think you must be right there."

Rozzy stood. The effort it took to play this charade exhausted her when inside she longed to crawl back to Rafe's arms. "Mrs. Allred is throwing a dance tonight. Do come, Henry?"

He took her hand and squeezed. "Perhaps I will."

Rozzy nodded gratefully and let him lead her from the room and to the door. She couldn't press too much too soon, but perhaps by this evening Henry would be willing to patch things up. Word wouldn't travel from Little River quicker than that, would it?

Rozzy pursed her lips as Mrs. Allred's driver opened the door of the Packard sedan. She wouldn't put it past Mrs. Van Doren to call up Rozzy's mother personally with the news.

Rozzy stared in awe at what must be over fifty of Mrs. Allred's closest friends, gathered in the dining room—cleared of furniture—and spilling into the adjoining hall and library for the dance. She had yet to spot Henry, which unnerved her and made her stomach pinch at the thought that his mother had talked him out of coming, but she held out hope.

The only space available for the band to set up was in the sitting room at the front of the house, its doors to the library also thrown open to allow the music to permeate every corner of the lower floor. Rozzy's parents had danced their fair share, and Mother paraded Daddy around to all the acquaintances she had in town, beaming at the women exclaiming over her handsome husband and no one ruining the occasion with any talk of their separation. At least not that Rozzy had heard, and not in front of her mother either, since she still glowed with pride.

True to her word, Mrs. Allred had invited plenty of younger gentlemen for Rozzy to flirt with, and she hadn't so much as moved from one room to the next without a young man at her side the entire evening. Though her thoughts strayed to Rafe and whatever he might be doing at the moment (likely sleeping, considering the lateness of the hour), she did her best to smile, laugh at the men's jokes, and pretend interest in their talk of cars, baseball, and business. And worry that Henry wouldn't come.

"You look as though you could use a little extra breathing room, Rosaline." A voice near her snapped her attention back to the conversation she shared with a group of people around her age.

She turned, with profound relief, to see Henry at her side. "Is that possible?" she asked, snatching up his arm and drawing close to him.

Henry chuckled. "The porch is not very crowded, only a couple or two. The wind is blowing a little, so most of the women prefer to stay inside so they don't upset their hair." He weaved through groups of people as he led her through the hall and then the entryway. "You don't mind, do you?" He winked.

"No, I don't mind a little wind." For the first time all night, Rozzy's nerves eased. Rafe would've thought to extricate her from this mess of people too. And Henry had come. Perhaps her plan wasn't lost. Her fingers fluttered to her hair and the twists Mrs. Allred's maid had fixed for her. What Rozzy wouldn't give to undo the pins, set aside the sparkling headband across her forehead, and let the wind toss her hair. It might be almost like riding Irene.

When they escaped the confines of the stuffy house, only one other couple stood on the porch. The wind Henry spoke of was a slight breeze in Rozzy's opinion, working a few hairs loose so they tickled her cheeks. Henry left her side to retrieve something to drink, so Rozzy reveled in the moment alone, leaning up against the bright white railing and taking a deep breath.

The air tasted like motorcars, nothing like the fresh pine-and-sage-brush scent of home. Even closing her eyes couldn't bring to mind the sound of Irene's hooves pounding the dirt or the swish of tall grass. Laughter and music surrounded her, pushing out the solace Rozzy wanted most.

Then the lightest breath of pine scent wafted by, and her thoughts swung to sparkling blue eyes and a choir-boy smile. To the way his hat sometimes slipped down low over his forehead and the way he made words so pretty and interesting when he spoke.

"Here you go, baby."

Rozzy's eyes flew open to find Henry standing beside her. The pine scent she'd detected was his aftershave. He held out a glass of punch to her, which she took, and she hoped the darkness covered the heat of a blush in her cheeks. "Thank you." She took a sip, unsure if the heat from her blush had spread or if the crush of the guests inside still stifled her.

To her surprise, the drink stung her throat, and she coughed and sputtered. Henry whipped a handkerchief from his pocket, which she used to dab the front of her dress. Her mother would be mortified if she'd seen.

"Is this alcoholic?"

"Yes." Henry raised his brows at her surprise, setting down both their drinks on the rail beside them.

"Golly, isn't that illegal?" Rozzy said, her voice hoarse from the confrontation with the punch.

He suppressed a chuckle and leaned close. He took the handkerchief from her hand and used it to dab at her cheek. "I'll go get you something different if you prefer not to drink."

"Well, of course I don't drink." In an effort to cover her embarrassment at his nearness, her words carried an edge. She dropped her voice. "Don't you think Mrs. Allred is worried about her home being raided? Suppose someone should find out she's serving that here?" Did Mother know? Rozzy didn't suppose she'd approve of her friend's choice of refreshment.

He grinned at her. "I won't tell if you won't." He winked. His expression softened at her shock, and he took her hand gently in his. "You don't have to drink."

She arched an eyebrow at him. "Of course I won't. But suppose the police arrive?"

Henry pressed his lips together and turned away, but it didn't fool her. He was trying to hold back a laugh. Her cheeks stung with heat again. "I don't think there's any danger of that. I'm sure all this liquor has been in Mrs. Allred's cellar, and there's no law against drinking what you already own. Just against buying it." A moment later, he turned back to her, his expression composed again. "In any case, my car is very fast. We can escape quite quickly should the police show up. It might be sort of exciting, even. I don't suppose anything like that ever happens in Wyoming?"

She laughed, chasing away her embarrassment yet again. "No. The last thing that chased me was—" And she'd gone so long without thinking of Rafe that time. At least five minutes.

"Yes?" Henry's brows furrowed in confusion.

"My neighbor's dog, but only because I had one of her puppies and she didn't like me taking it so far from her." Rozzy looked down and traced a finger along the edge of the railing. "Is that why you're really backing out, Henry? Do you think life would be too dull there?" she asked.

"I don't know the first thing about being a cowboy," Henry said, picking back up his glass and swirling the liquid but not drinking. He stared into the glass, and his reluctant expression worried Rozzy.

She took the glass from him, setting it down so she could take his hand. "I'll teach you. You know how to ride a horse, don't you?"

He chuckled. "Passably, I suppose."

"That's the perfect start. I think you'd look rather swell in a cowboy hat." When she tried to picture it, however, only Rafe's smiling face would come to her mind, with his hat tilted up on top of his head as he gazed at her.

Henry took a hand away to brush her cheek with his thumb. "Rosaline?"

"Everyone calls me Rozzy," she said, staring at his chest, her insides squirming like one of Queenie's puppies. "Now don't let my mother hear you, but I'd like it if you did." Still, she couldn't look at him.

He tilted her chin up to force her. He frowned, and she realized he mirrored the expression from her face. "Rozzy?" he asked in a quiet voice.

"Marry me, Henry. Please?" She almost choked on the words, and not because they were so frightfully bold. She'd never even asked a man to dance, but she had to get this over with. Get Henry to agree. Get Rafe and his kisses out of her mind somehow.

Still, Henry frowned. He was a clever man, though he never put his wits to much use. She supposed he must suspect her true feelings, but she pleaded anyway.

"You know I will," he said after a long moment. "But I have to convince Mother."

Her muscles should loosen. Happiness should course through her that he'd saved her. But her throat tightened more, so she had to clear it before saying, "Must you? Suppose we run off."

Henry laughed. He did have a nice laugh, she thought. Smooth, not jarring or annoying. And he was handsome, with shining dark hair and dark eyes. All in all, a fair catch. "Without my mother," Henry said carefully. "I don't even have the money for a license."

"I'll pay for it," Rozzy reminded him, though she hated to point out that she could pay when he couldn't.

He brushed back some of the hair from her face. "Yes, I know," he said quietly. Then he forced a smile. "Have you had enough fresh air?"

"I don't think that's possible—to have enough fresh air." She shrugged at him, pretending it didn't bother her so much not to have more fresh air and more wide-open space. Denver felt quite claustrophobic.

"Do you fancy a dance, baby?"

Oh, she would have to break him of that habit. "Darling" sounded so much better—well, when Rafe said it, anyway. So maybe she'd better let Henry keep on calling her that. It wouldn't do any good to fall in love with her husband, much as she wouldn't mind being friends. "Yes, I would."

It had been such a long night. Rozzy yawned hard as she mounted the stairs, listening as the last of Mrs. Allred's guests bid her good night, Henry among them. He'd kissed the top of her hand when he'd said goodbye and promised to call in the morning with news of his mother's answer, to which Rozzy had frowned.

"Be patient," he'd whispered, grinning. "I'll steal you away if she doesn't come around in a jiffy."

"Thank you, Henry," she'd answered, full of genuine gratitude. But she had to convince him to work fast. She and her mother had spent the last two days shopping, and Rozzy let her mother buy all sorts of clothes Rozzy would never need. She hadn't the will to put up a fight over them. Besides, she needed Mother in high spirits for when she found out that Rafe had jilted her—which was perhaps not a fair term, considering she hadn't planned to marry him in the first place. But after that kiss . . . well, she felt jilted no matter what. In any case, at the rate Mother was purchasing everything possible, they'd have all Rozzy's things within the week and be headed back to Wyoming before she'd convinced Henry.

Her parents had gone upstairs just ahead of her, so she didn't hurry after them. A moment alone with Daddy would lead to more questions and probing into how serious Rozzy was about marrying Henry. Mother would want to discuss further the clothes they had bought and what Rozzy should wear to what event when the wedding festivities began, and every minute she beamed over planning her daughter's wedding was another minute that Rozzy couldn't bear to tell her the truth.

But she wasn't slow enough. As she came up the stairs, she glimpsed them standing outside their bedroom—Mrs. Allred had put them in one, for appearance's sake, Mother claimed to Rozzy. Rozzy had smiled at the mild protest. They were married, after all, and Rozzy would never question the rare occasion when she felt they were truly a family again.

She hesitated, ducking to sit on the stairs in hopes of avoiding them both and sneaking off to her own room once they went inside theirs, but it seemed they were in no hurry.

"You were quiet during the supper this evening," Mother said, her voice leaning toward sulky.

"Have you forgotten I'm just a cowboy, Matty? I'm as out of place in your high society as I've ever been." Daddy's voice sounded resigned and weary.

"Well." Mother's tone pitched shrill in haughtiness, and Rozzy sighed and hoped they took their argument into the bedroom rather than make a scene that the guests lingering in Mrs. Allred's entryway would overhear. "You certainly fooled me all those years ago."

But Daddy just laughed. "The fact that you married me is a testament to that. Of course I played the part of the gentleman you wanted—the battle to win your heart was a blasted long affair, and I had to resort to fighting dirty."

Rozzy lifted her hand to her lips to cover a snicker, although the sweetness of the words made her sigh along with her mother. Neither spoke for several moments, and when Rozzy raised her head to see if they'd gone inside their room, she found her parents kissing—right in the hallway, where anyone could see.

She slumped down again and leaned against the railing with a smile. She didn't get her hopes up. She had witnessed the ups and downs of her parents' marriage too much over the last ten years to put much stock in them kissing, but even she had to admit that Daddy seemed to be giving up long-fought-over territory—he had come all the way to Denver with them! Rozzy could count the number of times he'd made that journey and endured society for Mother's sake on only two fingers, both times back when Rozzy was young.

What she wouldn't give to have Rafe next to her right now. Her hopes rose, hopes her parents were bound to disappoint one way or another. Back when Daddy had first moved back to his homestead, she'd prayed every time she saw them together that they'd make up and he'd come home. It always ended in a fight.

Which ended in Rafe comforting her. Even after she'd given up her childish dreams that they'd mend fences. What would Henry think of her parents living apart? Did he know? Mother had probably not spoken candidly with Mrs. Granger about the living arrangements, given her friend's strict propriety, but there had to be talk. Daddy hardly ever came to Denver with Mother, even back in the days he'd lived at the Big House. Would Henry understand the way Rafe did? Of course he wouldn't.

"I thought you'd outgrown your spying days."

Daddy's voice surprised her, and she shot to her feet. "What are you doing back downstairs?" she asked. At least they'd finished their embarrassing display before Mrs. Allred came up, though Rozzy couldn't be sure how long it had lasted, given that she'd been lost in her thoughts—

again. She hadn't been able to concentrate for two minutes together since leaving Little River.

"Matty wants a glass of warm milk," Daddy said. "I've come down to instruct on how it's to be done, though I doubt they'll get it right. Mrs. Hewitt has a secret recipe, I think." He leaned in to kiss Rozzy on the forehead before he passed by. "Did you have a good evening?"

Rozzy put her hands on her hips. "What's gotten into you?" she asked with narrowed eyes.

He laughed and put his arm around Rozzy's shoulders. "I've been stubborn for too long, and when my daughter got engaged, I realized I'd let too many years slip away fighting over silly things. I love your mother, little miss. I really do."

She buried her head in his shoulder, irritated at the emotion swelling within her, because it had nothing to do with her father's tender admission and all to do with the possible double meaning of his statement. "You've gone soft," she mumbled, because she couldn't admit to him that her quarrel with Rafe wasn't over something silly—that choosing Rafe was tantamount to giving up her dreams of running the Arrow C, no matter what anyone said. Rafe wasn't a woman, and he couldn't understand how he would take the ranch from her whether he meant to or not. And she may be naïve in many things, especially when it came to city life, but not enough to believe that a trip to Denver and some stolen kisses in a hallway meant a fairy-tale ending for her parents, whatever sentimental things Daddy spouted. Too many times they'd disappointed her on that score, like she and Rafe would if she gave in and married him.

Daddy leaned back and used his finger to tilt her chin up. "Do you love him?" he asked in a low voice.

She backed away a step. He didn't understand either. She did. So much, and that was the problem. "It doesn't matter."

He sighed, reminding Rozzy of his resigned tone from before. "It does if you love him enough," he said, and he gave her a knowing nod before he hurried on down the stairs.

As she watched him stop in the hall to chat with Mrs. Allred about the warm milk, Rozzy thought of Henry. Wouldn't marrying a man like him mean less work for her? He would never interfere, and neither

Daddy nor Papa Ed would ever allow him to. She wouldn't have to choose between marrying to please her mother and keeping the ranch. Best of all, they could live on friendly terms. She could give Henry the freedom he didn't have while he was dependent on his parents.

But how could she call a life without Rafe easy at all?

# CHAPTER 15

The hammer fell the next morning at luncheon. Mrs. Allred's housekeeper called Mother away to take a phone call from Wyoming, and Rozzy hoped that some disaster at the ranch house had made it imperative that Mrs. Hewitt talk with Mother right away.

Mother returned to the table, her expression tense, dashing Rozzy's hopes. Mother cast a look at Rozzy and said, "That was Mrs. Van Doren."

Rozzy's fingers went cold, for the biggest gossip in Little River making a long-distance call to Denver could only mean that the rumors Rafe had threatened to let spread had begun. She abandoned her meal. "She was well, I hope," Rozzy said, scooting her chair backward.

"Practically giddy," Mother responded with her teeth locked in a gruesomely false smile.

"I see," Rozzy said. "I hope you don't mind if I excuse myself." She skedaddled without looking back.

She found the telephone in Mrs. Allred's library and placed a long-distance call herself to the ranch house at the Double A.

"He's not here, Miss Pender," Mrs. Cowles said in a terse tone, and Rozzy nearly cried. Rafe's housekeeper hadn't once called her "Miss

Pender" since coming to work at the Double A five years before. "He went out on the range hours ago."

"I see." Rozzy kept her tone polite, though she longed to snap at the housekeeper for this unfair treatment. Rozzy was looking out for Rafe, saving them both from heartache that would eventually come. "When he comes in for lunch, would you have him phone me at Mrs. Allred's in Denver?"

"I'll tell him, miss. But there's no saying if he will or not." The haughtiness in Mrs. Cowles's voice could rival any tone of Mother's.

So Rozzy used the same tactic she would if she were talking to her mother: stubbornness. "Well, you let him know I'll keep calling until I reach him."

"Yes, Miss Pender," she snapped.

"And good heavens, must you really call me that just because Rafe's angry with me?" Rozzy found her tone quite pathetic. Everything kept heaping up. A few weeks ago, not marrying Rafe seemed like a simple thing, but with every hour came another thing taken from her if she didn't. Mrs. Cowles's friendship was just another in a long list.

"I'd call this a sight more than angry, Miss . . . Rozzy." At least Mrs. Cowles's voice softened. "Never seen a fellow more down than you left the boss."

Rozzy blinked rapidly to keep her emotion at bay. "Well, it hasn't been a picnic for me, Mrs. Cowles."

"You know how to fix that. You can't do better than the boss, if you don't mind me saying so."

"I'm well aware." Rozzy swiped at her eyes and held the phone away so she could sniff discreetly. Mrs. Cowles and Daddy made it sound so easy. Sure, it seemed simple. Marry Rafe. Live happily ever after with the man she loved. Things weren't likely to work out that way.

"I'll give him your message, miss." Mrs. Cowles's voice had returned to the normal, sweet tone she had adopted with Rozzy about five minutes after they'd first met. Mrs. Cowles was young, too young to be a widow with three young boys.

"Thank you," Rozzy said with as much warmth, and she hung up the phone.

When she turned around, she found her mother standing in the doorway, her arms folded and one red-and-black André Perugia shoe tapping the marble floor. "Would you care to explain why Rafe told the Van Dorens at dinner yesterday evening that he had called the engagement off?" Mother asked, and then she pressed her lips into a thin, angry line as she awaited the answer.

Rozzy squared her shoulders and swallowed back the lump in her throat. "Because he has."

Mother took a step closer, concern replacing the irritation on her features. "Truly, it was Rafe?" she asked, confusion in her tone. "Why would he do that? I know you think I forced him to propose to you—"

"You did," Rozzy pointed out, twisting her hands together.

"Rafe has loved you for a long time. I only . . . urged him to speak sooner than he may have." Mother took another step closer, reaching to take Rozzy's hand.

"I know." Rozzy closed her eyes. "He said so right before he called off the wedding."

Now Mother took Rozzy in her arms. "Rosaline, darling," she said softly, stroking Rozzy's back.

Hearing that he had truly done what he had threatened to affected her more than she had expected. She had been trying since the day it happened to wriggle out of her engagement to Rafe, yet deep down perhaps she had known she never really wanted the problem solved. Perhaps deep down she had realized how much she loved him—perhaps even when she was fourteen and had spent days crying because he'd left her for college.

"Don't you worry," Rozzy said, squaring her shoulders and pulling from her mother's grasp. "I've convinced Henry to renew our engagement."

Mother scoffed and raised an eyebrow.

"And he's agreed that if his mother doesn't come around, why, we'll just run off together."

Mother rolled her eyes. "When Rafe calls back, you'd do best to straighten things out between you. You'd be a lot happier if you gave up on Henry and followed your heart." She wagged a finger at Rozzy.

"That's just it—as much as I'd like to, I can't straighten it out. Forgive me, Mother, but all I've ever wanted was to run the Arrow C—"

Mother clenched her jaw but took a deep breath. "Marrying Rafe won't change that."

"Oh, you of all people should see that it will! That's what you hoped when you figured on marrying me off to him. Papa, Daddy, you— everyone wants me to marry Rafe so they can see the Arrow C safely in a man's hands, and that's what will happen. Rafe says he'd never take the ranch from me, but he won't have much of a choice if you all have your way. How can I choose between the love I've known all my life and the one I've just discovered?" Rozzy slumped into a rose-colored velvet armchair next to the desk and put her head in her hands.

Mother's response held shockingly little sympathy. "I, of all people —as you say—know best that loving a *place* will never be as satisfying as loving a *person*."

"It's not that simple," Rozzy moaned through her fingers.

"I'll tell you what is, then."

Rozzy's head snapped up at what she routinely described as her mother's cowgirl voice—a bit of country twang and a hard tone. She used it so rarely, it always got Rozzy's attention.

"You are a Nickel woman. You can sit here crying, or you can get up and realize there is a way for you to get exactly everything you want." Mother nodded with a resolute snap and then turned and strode from the room.

HENRY RETURNED that afternoon to take Rozzy on a drive to Rose Acres, west of Denver. "I thought you might like to leave the city behind for an hour or two," he said as he opened the door for her to climb inside his black Mercedes convertible.

"Oh, I would like that." She tied a handkerchief over her hair, even though Henry had put the top on. It was such a pain to have to worry about keeping herself prim and proper all day long.

He was quiet as they drove, for which she was grateful. Her thoughts wound around her mother's declaration that Rozzy could have every- thing she wanted. But how could her mother advise her to marry Rafe? How could her mother promise that Rozzy could have a happy marriage? Especially if she married the love of her life, as Mother had done? It wasn't as though Mother hadn't demanded, over and over, that Daddy come home. Nickel woman or not, her demands hadn't stopped Daddy from doing exactly as he pleased.

"You must have a lot of thoughts stored up," Henry said as he pulled up to Rose Acres.

"Thank you for allowing me to sort them out." She reached over to lay a hand gratefully on his arm before he got out to get her door.

"My pleasure," he said when he opened it and offered his hand to her. She took it, and they made their way toward the gardens.

Breathing in the sweet rose scents did a lot to smooth out the tension in Rozzy's neck, and with each step, she found her arms swinging a little more and each breath a little deeper. "What a marvelous idea this was, Henry. Thank you."

"You're welcome, Ros—Rozzy." He tipped his hat at her, and she smiled, turning her attention back to the roses growing as far as the eye could see. All the greenery reminded her of home, and before long, her thoughts turned back to Rafe. Rozzy did appreciate the way Henry didn't intrude on their walk with words, how he seemed to know she wished to enjoy the beauty around her in silence.

But that silence meant thinking of Rafe. Of how there seemed no way out, despite what her mother said. *Everything you want.* What did that include for Rozzy? Running the Arrow C and a happy life with Rafe. It was the second that confused her most. She supposed, especially with Rafe's help, that she could outthink Papa and Daddy and keep the reins of the Arrow C firmly in her hands. But how could she marry Rafe and not ruin his life? Not ruin hers?

"Henry, may I tell you something?" she asked.

He started, embarrassing Rozzy for how long they'd walked along in silence. He wouldn't think her a good companion for that. "Of course," he said, donning a smile. His expression turned expectant and hopeful, which Rozzy wondered at.

"Though my parents have acted the part of a perfect family, my father hasn't lived with us for ten years." She sighed, the confession reminding her that no matter what her mother said, Rozzy's plight was hopeless.

Henry blinked at her a few times and then frowned. "That's odd. They looked quite in love at Mrs. Allred's party. In fact, a couple of fellows accused your father of acting as though he were a teenager again." Henry's frown melted, replaced with a chuckle.

"Yes," Rozzy said, shaking her head. "That did seem true last night and ever since—" She almost mentioned Rafe. "I can't quite explain it," she finished instead.

Henry's smile took on a paternal slant as he tilted his head at her. "Looked as though he couldn't live without her, if you ask me. Maybe it's just taken him a while to realize it." He stopped and turned to face her. "Rozzy, would you please be honest with me? Why do you want to marry me?"

Rozzy blinked at him, surprised at his blunt tone. Seriousness had crept into his expression a time or two, but ever since she'd known him, Henry had shown a lack of care for most things. It had reassured her over the three years of their understanding that the same attitude would apply to his interest in the ranch. "I have to," she admitted, heat swirling through her cheeks and down into her belly. "To save my reputation." But talk would die down soon enough, and she could weather that. "To please my mother," she added, getting nearer to the truth.

He took a step closer, looking down at her, that paternal expression turning a touch stern. "And?"

She drew in a long breath, staring up at him and hoping his interest would waver. He remained quiet, waiting for an answer. "You won't take my ranch from me," she whispered.

Henry nodded, and a smile—the most genuine she'd ever seen grace his expression—worked onto his lips. My, he could make some girl turn head over heels for that. "No. I won't," he said. "Which I've long suspected is why you chose me. An honor, no doubt, Rozzy," he teased, making her cheeks burn like the devil himself. "You are well aware that I have my own reasons for marrying you. And I will, if you'd like me to." He reached for her hands, gripping them in his. "But baby, be careful you do not make the same mistake your parents have."

# CHAPTER 16

When Rozzy returned from her drive with Henry, she put in another call to Little River right away. It seemed an eternity before the operator connected her with the Double A ranch house, and the moments between when Mrs. Cowles answered and handed the phone over to Rafe lasted at least two days.

"Good afternoon, Miss Pender," he greeted her.

"Oh, stop it," she said, her temper already rising at his insistence on acting so formal with her. She couldn't remember a time Rafe was mad enough at her to call her that. He'd been formal during his proposal, but only because Mother had insisted. "You don't need to sound as though you've smelled manure in your bedroom just because you must speak to me." She couldn't help that his cold tone made her stomach twist into uncomfortable knots, not to mention the way it clogged up her throat. Yet at the same time, that voice, though brittle with strain, made her believe everything could be okay. Even if she didn't quite see how at the moment.

He didn't change his tone at all when he said dryly, "Mrs. Cowles said you'd called. I'm sorry I missed it."

"Yes, I called," she snapped. "How dare you spread all around town that we aren't getting married." Her temper kept rising with every icy word he said, and Rozzy was forced to admit that perhaps she was more like her mother than she had ever wanted to admit. "You're going to be mighty embarrassed."

Rafe's tone fired up. "I believe we have already discussed my feelings on the town talking about me."

"We have," Rozzy retorted. Words flew to her tongue. Henry's advice and honesty spurred her on like a whip cracked over a team of horses. "But the fact of the matter is, Rafe Adams, that I'm going to marry you whether you like it or not."

AT ROZZY'S INSISTENCE, they rode the train back to Little River as soon as possible. And the moment they stepped off, she had Bert drive her and Mother over to Mrs. Plummer's house, a request that Mother supported with a smug smile and no other comment but to say to Bert, "Yes, I know it's nearly nine. We've phoned ahead." Rozzy would have preferred to hear, "I told you so."

"Come in, come in," Mrs. Plummer said when she answered the door. "I was quite surprised to get your call. What could be so urgent, Mrs. Pender?"

"This was my idea," Rozzy said apologetically. She took two folded papers from her beaded handbag. She smoothed out the first and handed it to Mrs. Plummer.

"What's this?" Mrs. Plummer looked over the picture of the white silk voile dress with stars embroidered on the bodice and the swishy skirt that included nine panels.

"If it's not too much trouble, I'd like that instead of the other one we picked out." Rozzy bowed her head and fidgeted with the belt of her dress.

Mrs. Plummer blinked in surprise. "This is quite different from your original request." She cast Mother a confused frown.

"Yes. Rosaline has had a change of heart. I'm quite sorry for the extra work we've given you, but we'll pay in full for both dresses."

When Rozzy looked up, she caught Mother and Mrs. Plummer staring at each other, each with their lips quirked as though they couldn't help but laugh. As though both women had known that eventually, Rozzy would come around and start to care very much about the dress she would wear when she walked down the aisle to Rafe.

"What are you going to do with two wedding dresses, Miss Rosaline?" Mrs. Plummer asked, her thin gray eyebrows rising high on her forehead.

Rozzy squared her shoulders and raised her head. "You know how my mother is. I'm sure she'll find some event I can wear the other to." None of the women could keep straight faces at that point, and their laughter broke out. To hear these women believe in her made the future seem attainable.

Mrs. Plummer came forward and patted Rozzy on the cheek. "You'll get married in whatever your heart desires, darling, if I have to stay up all night to sew."

Rozzy caught the woman's hand before she pulled it away, squeezing it with gratitude. Her mother had once said that the people of this town would tear her reputation down if given the chance—but they would also circle the wagons around her if asked. Well, everyone but maybe Tillie Van Doren. "Do you think you could manage a veil like this one?" Rozzy asked, handing Mrs. Plummer the second paper.

"I've no doubt." Mrs. Plummer nodded firmly as she studied the paper. Her frown returned, and she chewed on her lip when she raised her gaze. "There're rumors in town that there won't be a wedding after all."

Rozzy swallowed. Her mother pressed her lips together but nodded at Rozzy.

"You leave those rumors to me, Mrs. Plummer," Rozzy said.

THOUGH SHE WOULD HAVE LIKED to instruct Bert to head to the Double A without a minute to lose, it was too late for Rozzy to go over and see Rafe. She tossed and turned most of the night, despite how comfortable it was to sleep in her own bed after so many nights away. What if Tillie and Bessie had already begun flirting with Rafe? Perhaps he'd reconnected with some girl he knew at college. She'd been gone for over a week. Anything could have happened, and if she lost Rafe to someone like Tillie, Rozzy could not live with it—whether she deserved it or not.

She rose early and spent far too long trying to replicate the twisty-turny way Mrs. Allred's maid had done her hair before she finally called on Mrs. Hewitt to do something proper with it. She worked on Rozzy's hair and hummed, creating such a piece of art that Rozzy vowed to take advantage of such talent more often.

"That's nice of you to say, miss, but I won't hold my breath. Before long, you'll have that ring on your finger and be back in the saddle with that horrid cowboy hat squashing your hair." Mrs. Hewitt laughed and winked at Rozzy.

Rozzy laughed with her, happy that some of the knots in her chest loosened a little at the action. "Well, I am pleased to know that at least my hair will do justice to the lovely wedding gown Mrs. Plummer is making me."

Mrs. Hewitt shook her head. "If your mother had known that all it would take to make you interested in your wedding was realizing you loved Mr. Rafe, she might have changed her tactic." She held up Rozzy's nicest day dress—a white linen frock with pretty red beads and two rose-colored flowers at the waist.

"I think I've known I loved him for a while," Rozzy said quietly. "Just wasn't sure what to do about it."

Mrs. Hewitt frowned. "What is that supposed to mean, missy?"

Rozzy waved her off. "Never mind. Love isn't as easy as people make it sound."

Mrs. Hewitt *hmm*-ed as she helped Rozzy into the dress. "No, it isn't. Weddings aren't happily ever afters. Takes work. You're a clever girl to realize that."

And even then, it didn't always go the way people planned. In fact, hardly ever. She thought more about her father's words. He'd said things would work out if she loved Rafe enough. Could that be what he had meant—that he had realized that his love for Mother meant more than the freedom he craved?

"Miss Rozzy?" Mrs. Hewitt questioned, and Rozzy snapped back to attention.

"Thank you," Rozzy said, smoothing over the skirt. "I appreciate your help."

Mrs. Hewitt made her own adjustments and then left the room with an affectionate pat on Rozzy's arm. Rozzy stared at the pretty girl before her in the mirror—the girl her mother had tried to dress her up as for years.

She reached for her hat and came down the stairs to get breakfast, surprised to see Daddy sitting at the table. She had assumed now that they'd come home and the guests had gone, he would return to his homestead. But he sat there having bacon and eggs in his suit, still looking the part of the gentleman. Like the man her mother had dreamed about.

"Good morning, Daddy." She leaned over and kissed him and then went to the sideboard for eggs and toast.

"I see your look, Miss Rozzy," he said in a faux-stern voice.

"I have no look." She smiled, her anxious mood lifting even more. Having Daddy come to Denver and now stay in the house gave her real hope that he had meant his declaration that he had wasted enough time fighting with Mother over the years. That there was truth to his idea that loving someone enough could make happiness possible with a little hard work.

"Good." He grinned and gave her a nod. "When your mother comes down, I'd like to take you two for a drive to show you something."

She furrowed her brows. "I had planned to go over to see Rafe this morning."

"As I gathered from your appearance." Daddy winked, causing Rozzy to blush deeply. "Hasn't your mother taught you that the appropriate calling time is in the afternoon?"

Still blushing, Rozzy shook her head. "Rafe hardly cares about that."

"Rafe is more than likely out working, Roz. You'll have to wait for this evening."

She slumped because her father was right. Rafe would be out on the range somewhere, and though she knew her way around the Double A, she would have to change out of this particular dress and ruin the lovely hairdo Mrs. Hewitt had created. And after her last meeting with Rafe, she needed every advantage.

"What is this surprise, then?" she asked, trying to work up more excitement since her father's eyes glittered with anticipation.

He simply smiled.

HER MOTHER WAS STILL SLEEPING, and after the long trip of the day before, she would likely sleep much longer. Since Rozzy had dressed up special, she figured she might as well get some use out of all Mrs. Hewitt's hard work while she waited around, so she had Bert drive her into town to fetch some things for Mrs. Hewitt.

She stopped by Mrs. Plummer's shop to make sure the seamstress didn't need any extra measurements after Rozzy had changed the order, and as she left, she came upon Tillie and Bess coming up the sidewalk.

"Well, so you're back, Rosaline," Tillie cried in mock glee. She hurried forward and took Rozzy's hands in hers. "How was Denver, you poor dear? Have you cancelled your dress order?" Tillie tilted her head toward the door Rozzy had exited. She didn't give Rozzy any time to answer. "Why, I never thought Rafe the coldhearted type, but he relayed the end of your engagement like he was reading from the phonebook."

Rozzy had the urge to let loose a string of words her mother would not approve of, but she pinched her lips shut for several seconds before answering. "Simply a misunderstanding." She pulled her hands away from Tillie and moved her clutch in front of her, hoping it would protect her from more of Tillie's supposed sympathy.

"Another one?" Tillie arched an eyebrow.

"Every couple has a spat or two," Rozzy excused, her jaw aching from clenching it to keep back all the nasty remarks she wished to make. She moved for the car Bert had parked at the curb.

"Especially in your family, dear." Tillie linked her arm through Rozzy's and frowned, the understanding pout of hers falling flat thanks to the smirk she couldn't quite banish. "I'll be sure to put in a word for you this evening."

"This evening?" Rozzy froze on the sidewalk, her thoughts of escaping Tillie disappearing as she turned to the young lady. Rozzy had heard that Rafe dined with the Van Dorens while she was in Denver, but she'd pushed the thought aside, not considering him in any danger of falling prey to Tillie.

"Oh, well, this is embarrassing, dear. I thought you knew. Rafe is taking me over to Gardenville for the dance. If you'd rather I didn't . . ." Tillie stroked Rozzy's arm that she still held, sighing as she nodded her condolences.

Even if Rozzy begged Tillie to break the date, she'd find some way to twist it and show Rozzy in a terrible light. She asked herself what Mother would do and then gave a light laugh. "I would hate to spoil your fun, Tillie. Go on ahead. I can't blame Rafe for getting his flirting out of his system, and who better to help with that than you?" She gave Tillie's hand a quick pat. "Good day," she called, pulling herself away before Tillie could react. Well, Tillie would be sure to tell Rafe how awful Rozzy was now. It was nearly worth it.

But once Bert drove away, she struggled to keep tears at bay. So Rafe had asked Tillie to a dance? Thoughts that Rafe would attempt to move on had occupied her mind, but she hadn't dwelled on them. Suppose Rafe didn't give her time to convince him to give her another chance?

"Knowing Miss Van Doren, she browbeat Rafe into taking her," Bert said from the front seat.

"Perhaps." Rozzy turned her gaze to the road as they left town, not comforted by his observation. Her Rafe wouldn't have let Tillie Van Doren browbeat him into anything.

She stared at the houses sliding by her view until they disappeared and turned into fields of beets and corn, and then Bert turned onto the road that led home. On one side, spreading toward the mountains, was the Arrow C. On the other side, the Double A. Two sides of her heart.

Bert pulled the car round to the front of the house when they returned, and Daddy escorted Mother down the steps. Rozzy smiled at the way her parents settled close to each other in the back seat, and she took the front with Bert.

He drove them up a winding road that led into the mountains. The barren, sagebrush-covered hills gave way to thick forests of pine trees that rose up like a tunnel on each side of them.

"Are we going on a picnic?" Rozzy turned to ask her father.

"Next time. I have something I'd like to show you." He gave her the enigmatic grin he'd been casting her since she'd returned from town and turned to look out the window. He and Mother held hands, and she leaned toward him, resting her chin on his shoulder as she followed his stare. They looked quite content with each other. It soothed Rozzy's bruised heart—until she remembered she might not get the chance to tell Rafe about it this evening, with him skipping off to Gardenville with Tillie.

Bert turned onto a rocky road, and the car bounced around so much Rozzy thought it might shake apart—or at least rattle out some of her teeth. She strained to see the coming landscape out the window, but the trees blocked the view. Still, she kept craning her neck, looking for what came next.

Then a house appeared in a break in the trees. It was simple in style, making it all the more beautiful. It was log, but the logs had been polished and stained a rich golden brown, glowing in the sunlight striking off its east wall. The bottom half was faced in rock of all shapes and sizes, probably scavenged from the land around it. Large, pristine windows gleamed back at them, and the whole sight captured Rozzy's gaze.

"Daddy . . ." Rozzy breathed at the same time Mother whispered, "What is this?" She leaned forward, gaping at the house, her eyes wide.

Daddy didn't answer, and Bert brought the car to a stop. Daddy helped Mother out of the car, but Rozzy didn't wait for Bert to come around for her before she shoved open the door and clambered out, eager to get a closer look. When she turned to question her father, she found him holding Mother's hand and watching her as she took in the sight, a gloved hand hovering over her mouth in wonder.

"You never wanted to live in that shack I built, darlin', and I have struggled to become the gentleman I must be to lord over that mansion of your father's. So I built you the dreams I always promised you." He used the hand he held to pull her closer to him and stared at her with an adoring look that made Rozzy quite sure he meant to live up to every word.

Mother turned to him and slapped him softly on the chest. "Oh, you old fool." Tears glistened in her eyes.

Daddy took that hand and pressed it against his chest. "Your fool, Matty. Always."

When he bent his head over Mother's, Rozzy turned away and wandered toward the stone steps that led to a polished door stained a dark brown. She gazed at the home, more convinced than ever that her father meant everything he'd said to her in Denver about making a new start with Mother. Had meant it for some time before he'd said it, by the look of things.

"Would you like to see inside?" Daddy asked from behind Rozzy, and she guessed they must be finished with their kissing business. She turned, amused at the delight in his face. It reminded her of the day he'd given her Irene. He'd led the horse right up to the porch, since Mother had insisted on dressing Rozzy in a nice dress for her birthday. When she'd placed her hands on the horse's velvety soft nose, Daddy had grinned so wide it made Rozzy giggle. She'd turned back to Mother, expecting to be scolded for getting dirty, but Mother had stared at Daddy, shaking her head and wearing a soft smile. He loved his girls. Anything to make them happy.

"Of course," Mother replied in a loving tone, taking his arm as they mounted the stone steps. Daddy opened and held the door for Mother and then turned to wait for Rozzy.

"You go on. It's Mother's house. I'll see it later," she said.

Daddy furrowed his brow, but she shooed him along with her hands, and he gave in with a shrug. It felt wrong reminding him that no matter what happened with Rafe, this wasn't a part of their life she'd follow them into. She belonged on the Arrow C. That was her home. And someone had to keep Papa Ed company in that big old house. Mother and Daddy would be fine in this pretty place without her.

The door opening again startled her, and when she looked up to see who had come out, she took a step back at the sight of Rafe. Her heart skittered. He wore dirty trousers—smudged with mud and who knew what else—and a stiff, dark blue work shirt, sleeves rolled up to his elbows. He smirked as he left the house, probably thinking many of the same things Rozzy did about those two old sweethearts. Did it give him hope for him and Rozzy?

He stopped on the top step when he noticed her, pushing back his cowboy hat as he always did when he got flustered and rubbing his forehead. "Didn't realize you were here too."

"Why are *you* here?" Rozzy asked, flustered herself. She squeezed the sides of her skirt, trying to figure out something to do with her hands. "You knew about this house?"

He nodded. "Well, for a few weeks. He told me about it after . . ." He let the words trail off, and he looked away, squinting at the sun overhead and then the trees around them, anywhere but at her. Probably after he and Rozzy had gotten engaged, when Daddy had expected Rafe to be his son-in-law. "He telegrammed ahead to ask me to make sure everything was ready for Mrs. Pender to see it this morning. He couldn't wait another second."

Rozzy scuffed her shoe along the dirt in front of her until she remembered they cost quite a lot and stopped. "He told me while we were in Denver that he meant to make things right. After ten years of their fighting, I guess I wasn't sure what to believe until I saw this."

Both their gazes turned back to the house again, a solid testament to Daddy's abiding love for Mother, even when it hadn't seemed like he cared enough to change.

Rozzy took a deep breath and forced herself to look up at Rafe. He hadn't moved an inch from the top step, as though he was afraid to come too close to her. "Can we talk, Rafe?" she asked timidly. There had never been anything she couldn't tell him, and she hated the hurt and awkwardness between them now, like the long fence that stretched between their two ranches, but higher and with no easy passage.

"Sure." He shrugged but still wouldn't make eye contact. What she wouldn't give for him to scramble down those steps and grab her up in his arms like he had the day he'd kissed her. She'd say a lot of things differently if she could redo that conversation.

"I mean it when I say I'm gonna marry you," she blurted.

He met her gaze with a sad look and a shake of his head. "Shoot, Roz, I know you mean it, but I don't think you can convince me. I don't want to be second best to the Arrow C all my life." He leaned against the railing, staring at his dirty boots.

"Second best! What a thing to say!" She caught herself before she stomped her foot. "That's not how it is at all."

He arched an eyebrow at her and folded his arms across his broad chest. "You've only decided to marry me now because somehow or other you've gotten Big Ed and T.J. to promise to let you keep the ranch if you do."

"I have not," she stuttered, but the truth of the matter was she *had* meant to extract that exact promise. Had the words all worked up and examples enough to prove she knew as much about running this ranch as Rafe or anyone she might marry.

Rafe knew her well enough to shake his head and chuckle.

"It's just like you to laugh at a time like this," she snapped. "And you're being mighty unfair, don't you think? To make me choose between you and something I've wanted my whole life."

The amusement fell away from his face. "Is it unfair to ask that I be more important to you than that? That after promising to love you for eternity, to expect the same kind of loyalty I'd give you?" He came down the steps, taking them one at a time as he spoke, until he stood right in front of her, making her breath stop at the depth of the heartache in his eyes. It wrung Rozzy out to witness him hurting, reminding her of the night they'd fought to save the puppies. How desperate he'd been over something he loved.

"I'll love you just as long," she said in a quiet voice. "But you're saying I have to give up the Arrow C to prove it?"

He pushed his hat back down on his head, casting his face into shadow. Pulling away from her. "I know I can't ask that of you." He shoved his hands into the pockets of his pants and walked past her.

Rozzy had been fool enough to believe her mother about keeping the Arrow C and Rafe, about having all she wanted, about ending up happy. Though maybe that delusion had been wishful thinking on her own part. So Daddy had built Mother a home? It'd taken him ten miserable years to come to that.

"I was right all along," she muttered.

Rafe whirled, his eyes full of fire she'd never witnessed in him. It only made her surer of the conclusion she'd come to long ago.

She marched over to stand face to face with him. "I knew this is what love does to people." Then she walked past him to the empty car, leaving him standing there staring after her. She didn't know where

Bert had gone, but she was glad he hadn't stuck around to witness the tears welling in her eyes as she slammed the car door.

Given how angry and hurt Rafe had seemed over her words, it took longer than she'd expected before the rumble of his truck broke the silence of the forest. When he pulled around the house, she turned so she wouldn't accidentally catch a glimpse of him. Then she dropped her head in her hands and let loose a sob of frustration.

# CHAPTER 17

Rozzy saddled up Irene as soon as they returned. In the last few weeks, the only place she'd found peace was on top of her horse. But the fence line she rode along reminded her of days spent with Rafe, and loneliness hung over her. Searching the fence for places in need of repair didn't distract her enough from Rafe's words, from his hurt, from the feeling that she could ride along the fence line of their feelings and never find all the places she needed to fix.

Mother came up to Rozzy's room that night as she dressed for bed, looking sheepish but happier than Rozzy could remember in a long while. She sat down in one of the floral-covered tub chairs Rozzy had clustered near the window. "What do you think of our new home?" she asked, her expression bright with anticipation. She leaned an elbow on one of the arms of the chair and rested her head in her hand, the lace on the sleeve of her dressing gown draping down on the arm. She had crossed one leg over the other, and her foot tapped out a bright rhythm in the air.

"It's quite beautiful." Rozzy set down the brush she'd been using and turned from her vanity to face her mother, not quite sure how to broach the subject that she didn't intend to move there.

Mother and Daddy had made plans for them to move there as soon as possible as they'd driven back from the home to the Arrow C, Mother growing more excited by the second over the furniture she'd buy, who she might consult for the right look, what she might bring from the mansion, and where she'd find the perfect outdoor furniture for the wide porch. And would Daddy mind too much if she threw a party to show the whole town and all her friends? It hadn't surprised Rozzy at all that her father had agreed to the plan without any argument. He had turned over such a new leaf that Rozzy felt a little dizzy over it. She'd only been asked to comment from time to time, and exclamations of "that sounds neat!" and "I quite agree!" had proven sufficient. Her parents had held hands and stared at each other with stars in their eyes the whole way back to the ranch house. Rozzy couldn't remember a time either of them had behaved so lovesick.

"You've been quiet all day," Mother said, sitting up in the chair and leaning more toward Rozzy. "Haven't you smoothed things over with Rafe yet?"

Rozzy hated that everything in her chest pinched together and made it difficult to speak. She shook her head, feeling again her defeat. And hopelessness. She couldn't give up the one thing she'd worked her whole life for. She couldn't give up the one person who made her whole. She couldn't reconcile any of it with the knowledge that with or without Rafe, she was destined for a life of unhappiness.

Mother stood and crossed the short space between them to rub Rozzy's back softly. "What has he done?" she asked.

"He says he'll always be second best to the ranch in my eyes, and I don't see any way to make him see otherwise unless I tell him I'll give up the ranch. How can he make me choose? He knows how long I've wanted to run this ranch. It's so much a part of me, I don't even know if I'd be the same person without it." She raised her head and took a deep breath. It fueled more tears to roll down her cheeks rather than staving them off. "But I'm not the same person without Rafe either. You said I could figure out a way to have both, Mother, but thinking so only seems to have made the whole mess even worse."

Mother placed her hands on Rozzy's cheeks and kissed her forehead, smiling in a wistful way. "I suppose if I hadn't meddled, it might have turned out better."

The statement shocked Rozzy so much she began laughing, and through her muddled tears, she shook her head and said, "That's not helpful in the least."

Mother's grin widened, and she chuckled herself. "I know."

"It's all right, since nothing you could say would make any difference anyhow. I went and fell in love with him, and that's the biggest problem of all." Rozzy's laughter died, and her shoulders slumped. She might have married Henry Granger without realizing how much she loved Rafe. She might have found some happiness in ignorance.

"What in the world does that mean, you silly girl?" Mother asked, her fingers fluttering around the base of her neck as she eyed Rozzy with confusion. She put her hands on Rozzy's shoulders, lifting her and guiding her to the bed, where they could sit together.

"You of all people know how miserable love makes people," Rozzy cried. "I'm mighty glad you and Daddy have mended fences, but I've seen how awful it made you feel all those years, trying to win back his affection and make him come home."

"Oh, dear," Mother said in a whisper. She chewed on her lip, and her fingers curled around Rozzy's arm as tears welled in Mother's eyes. "I see I've meddled far more than I realized . . ." She sat in silence for several minutes, making anxious foals dance over Rozzy's chest. "I had hoped that by raising you strong and independent, I'd help you avoid the pitfalls of the mistakes in my own relationships." She sighed. "You see, you're partly right, I suppose, to say that love has caused the heartache between your father and me, but that is because I love him so much I could never let him go enough not to feel it."

"It makes Henry seem a more and more inviting prospect." Rozzy twisted her hands in her lap. The foals kicked out more discomfort at such traitorous words. Her heart was far too loyal to Rafe. Before she'd left Denver, she had told Henry as much. He had kissed her cheek and wished her the best.

"Miss Rozzy," Mother snapped in a tone that strangely made Rozzy more comfortable with the conversation. "You are clever enough to know that would bring with it its own form of heartache."

"Yes, Mama." She fell back onto the bed. "You see how impossible it all is?"

"Have you ever heard Big Ed say anything other than a sweet word about your grandmother?" Mother asked, her tone softening again and drawing Rozzy's gaze to her.

"Of course not." She'd been quite young when her grandmother died, but everyone at the ranch house talked about Grandmother in tones of the deepest love, from Bert to Mrs. Hewitt to Mother and Papa Ed.

"It's not out of any form of respect for the dead either, darling. It is, plain and simple, a true, deep love your grandfather had for her. That she had for him—enough to follow him from the comforts of their life out east to this brown wasteland—"

"Mama!" Rozzy sat back up in protest.

"I love it too, as much as you, but it is what it is. They never stopped loving each other, and despite some real hardships, they never fell to pieces the way your father and I did. I know we've done plenty of wrong —and plenty of wrong to you, little miss—but if you want a real example of what love is, you ought to look to that. Not to me." She reached over and pulled Rozzy into her arms, rocking her back and forth. "It's two examples of choosing. You and Rafe may well choose the better path—you're much smarter than T.J. and me."

Rozzy sat back, studying this bare piece of her mother's soul that had been offered, a peek beneath the tough exterior Mother had built to withstand the last ten years or more of storms. It shook Rozzy to the core. But then it left her with more hope than she'd felt since Rafe proposed. "Like you and Daddy are choosing now," she said in a quiet but firm voice.

"Oh yes, I hope we've gotten it right this time." The twinkle and giddiness returned to Mother's expression, and she reached over to clasp Rozzy's hands in hers once more. "It's only been a day, Rosaline. You're not giving up yet, are you?"

Determination joined the tight frustration in Rozzy's throat. Despite her mother's beautiful speech, no solutions presented themselves. "Rafe has as good as said nothing will convince him that he means more to me than the ranch—except giving it up, of course."

"Give it a little time, Rosaline," Mother said. "And don't call it quits after one conversation. Now *that* I know something about." She winked, and Rozzy rolled her eyes in impatience. She wanted a solution now.

Mother straightened and looked around the room. "I think your things will look very nice in the east bedroom at Rock Meadow. You've always loved sunrises."

"Rock Meadow?" Rozzy questioned instead of correcting her mother on the notion that she intended to move her furniture anywhere. If she wouldn't abandon this ranch for Rafe Adams, she certainly wouldn't for her parents.

"That's what your father has decided to call it, and I agree it's a wonderful name." Mother's giddy smile returned, and Rozzy lost any inclination to make it disappear—whether by continuing to discuss her predicament with Rafe or by explaining she wasn't moving to Rock Meadow.

"You and Daddy are agreeing on quite a lot these days," she said instead.

Mother wrapped her arms around Rozzy, and they nestled their heads together. She'd spent so long fighting against her mother on who she would become that the comfort that came from fighting on the same side filled Rozzy. "It's a nice change, isn't it?"

Well, on that, Rozzy could agree.

RAFE HAD JUST FINISHED INSTRUCTING Mrs. Cowles on some record keeping he had for her to do and had set out for the barn for his horse, when he caught sight of a familiar figure trotting up the road toward the house. He sighed, torn up inside. His need to see Rozzy was an ache like the kind that drove some men to drink. In even the few days since they'd spoken up at Rock Meadow—he still smirked inside at such a highfalutin name for something of T.J. Pender's—he missed her more fiercely than he had the two weeks she'd spent in Denver. He chalked that up to her change of heart and hearing that sweet voice say she'd love him as long as he would love her. But maybe the two-week separation could make the missing easier, and now every time he saw her again would increase the pain of missing her.

He watched her trot into the yard and dismount. Her hair, like the day he'd seen her at Rock Meadow, was done up into something more elaborate than usual, and she had her old cowboy hat tipped at an attractive angle that added mystery and sophistication to her features. It made her seem more grown up, even though she still wore her old brown trousers tucked into her cowboy boots and a simple white shirt with a brown button-up sweater on top—nothing like the delicate dress she'd worn when he'd seen her last.

"Good," she said as she strode toward him, holding Irene's reins loosely in her hands. "You haven't left. I never know if Mrs. Cowles is going to tell me where you are or not."

The half of him that insisted he must not keep on loving Rozzy scolded the I-can't-help-but-keep-on-loving-Rozzy half for wanting to laugh at how she spoke to him in the same old way. As though she hadn't a thought for the three times now that he'd told her things were through for them. As though she hadn't cut him in two by assuming he'd ever want to take her ranch from her. She turned that darned determination on winning him back. Rafe's heart would not weather this battle well. And one of the best generals in the county had taught Rozzy how to fight this fight—even if Matilda Pender had never seen a lick of real military action.

"Mrs. Cowles is not supposed to tell you anything about my whereabouts," he answered instead, "and if you knew what was good for the both of us, you'd quit pestering her and testing her loyalty."

"She's quite on my side, you know," Rozzy retorted, folding her arms and staring him down imperiously. "It's only because you pay her that makes her reluctant to disobey you." It should come as no surprise to Rafe that his employees ignored his instructions once she turned that sweet tone on them. He could hardly obey those instructions himself. "Anyway," she went on before he could word a proper reprimand, "I need you. Mother and Daddy are under the impression I'm moving up to Rock Meadow with them, and I haven't any idea how to tell them I'm not. You'd better come and help me."

"I've got work to do, Rosaline." He had taken to calling her that in his mind in an effort to loosen her hold, not that it worked much. It just made him picture her all done up like she'd been at their engagement party, which led to ideas of what she might have looked like coming down the aisle toward him and wondering if she would've worn a veil and a fancy dress or if she would have held on to her own simpler style.

"Don't you dare call me that," she snapped at him. "Being cross with me gives you no right to use that kind of language."

Rafe had to smash his hat down over his face to physically stop himself from smiling at her antics. He rubbed a hand over his face before righting his hat. "It might be better if you did live with them. If we had less interaction, it might make parting easier on us."

Rozzy rolled her eyes. "I don't intend to make anything easy on you, least of all living without me. And furthermore, if I really have lost you just because I want to run the ranch you spent half your life teaching me how to run, it's not likely I'll give it up simply because my parents have decided to live together again."

He shoved his hands in his pocket and took a step back, doing what he could to discourage her. Not that it would help if she had her mind set on something. He'd have to wait her out, as painful as she'd make it. During the entire conversation, Rafe had fought himself over his feelings for this exasperating woman, equal parts ready to strangle her, laugh with her, and berate her for the suffering she'd put him through.

That thought reminded him of how she'd worded her parting shot to him at Rock Meadow. "What did you mean about the kinds of things love did to people?" He'd thought a lot over her words, a sort of ache settling inside him the more he considered it.

Her cheeks turned a deep shade of pink, and she dipped her head, effectively hiding it under that cowboy hat. He thought about striding over to her and tipping her chin up to make her look at him, the way he might have a month ago without a second thought. But standing that close would make it darn near impossible not to stand closer still and kiss her.

"How it can make people all kinds of miserable." She lifted her head then, turning a pleading gaze on him with her pretty hazel eyes. Hazel eyes that had made his world turn for as long as he could remember. "That is," she went on, clearing her throat and raising her voice, "if we choose it."

He ground his teeth together. "Don't you put this on me, Miss

Rozzy," he grumbled, moving away. She had a choice too. Perhaps he'd made that unfair, but he had to mean more to her than a parcel of land, had to know she believed in him above all else. How could he ever be sure what came first in her life?

He strode by her, but not in time to miss the way she muttered, "Stubborn man." He headed toward the barn, intent on ignoring her.

But she turned and hurried after him, Irene plodding along in her wake. "Oh, I bet the puppies have gotten awfully big while I was gone, haven't they?"

He grunted in response, but it didn't deter her. She tied Irene up to a post outside the barn and then followed him right on in, making a beeline for the stall where Queenie was usually found with her offspring.

"Oh, they're still just as darling," Rozzy cooed as she gathered several into her arms and buried her face in their fur. Her enthrallment served to remind him of the night they'd raced to save the pups and the ensuing predicament it had caused. How that moment, when she'd woken up in his arms, he'd had a glimpse of the kind of bliss his future could hold.

He turned away from the reminder to ready his horse, hoping the puppy distraction would keep Rozzy occupied until he had left. However, it didn't surprise him that when he led his horse out of the barn, she kissed each of the puppies crowded in her arms and stood to follow. "I thought T.J. and your mother were on the brink of moving your furniture to the cabin," he said moodily. The more sensible side of him was losing the will to push her away, which meant he had better get her away before his sense went and deserted him completely and he started enjoying her company. Or worse, gave in to her logic about choosing whether or not love made him miserable.

"Nearly," she said, unconcerned. She untied Irene and hopped on in one smooth bound, waiting for him to mount as she looked down at him. "If they do get so far, I suppose I'll have to commandeer Jim to help me move it all back, and it will serve you right since you wouldn't come and keep it from happening in the first place."

Rafe turned to stare at her, wondering if she had always been so nonsensical. "You are maddening."

"I will continue to be so until you stop behaving so stubborn and patriarchal." She held his gaze without flinching, and staring into her eyes had him remembering the moment he had kissed her. Fire burned right up his belly and into his chest.

He flicked his reins at his horse's backside. "And now I am patriarchal?" he asked dryly.

"It seems you can't stand the idea of your wife running a bigger ranch than your own, so I don't know what else to call it." And she kept a straight face while saying it.

Rafe rolled his eyes and trotted out of the yard with her at his heels. His sensible side didn't even mind too much.

# CHAPTER 18

"How are things looking, little miss?"

Rozzy looked up at the sound of Papa Ed's voice approaching. "We'll round up the rest of the cows by tomorrow, and then the boys can start moving them." She turned back to the herd and shouted to get some of the straggling cows moving along.

"You riding along?" he asked.

"Get on!" she shouted instead of answering him right away, and then she squinted off into the distance. It was like leaving pieces of her soul behind thinking this way, but that was better than losing all of her heart. She might wear Rafe down over time when it came to marrying her, but at what cost to his love for her? Especially if she never showed him how important he was. He might always resent this ranch, and that would lead to making the kind of wrong choices Daddy and her mother had made over the years. She couldn't let that happen either.

But it twisted her up inside nonetheless. Threatened to keep her from doing what she had to do. She took a deep breath and pictured Rafe—the scruff on his chin the morning she had woken up next to him, the choir-boy smile that turned her upside down, the longing to be at his side even now when he pretended she was a nuisance.

"I got things I have to take care of here," she finally said.

Papa Ed flicked his reins and moved in closer to Rozzy. "Rafe keeping you awfully busy over at that ranch of his?" he teased.

She granted him a smile. Her days with Rafe had been successful, she thought. He didn't bark at her as much, and he'd stopped complaining about her showing up wherever he happened to be that day. It was progress. Now she had to tip the scales and prove she loved *him* above all else.

She cleared her throat and plowed on. "I think you ought to give the ranch to Daddy when you retire." She spit it out as quick as she could, worried she'd stop the words before she got it all out. *I can't live without Rafe,* she reminded herself.

Papa Ed pulled his horse in front of Rozzy's and came to a stop, forcing her to as well. "Your father doesn't want my ranch."

Convincing him that he must take it had been the second-hardest conversation of Rozzy's life. Mother had clucked that it shouldn't be necessary, but both Daddy and Rozzy had hushed her. "I've spoken to him already, and I think you'll find him more willing now."

Papa Ed guided the horse around so that he could face her, leaning over his saddle horn and resting his arms there. "This what you want, darlin'?"

She kept her shoulders straight and her head high. She owned this decision, no matter what it cost. But it didn't stop emotion from building in her chest and stuffing up her head as she stared out at the sea of cows before her. "I'll ... hopefully ... have the Double A—to help Rafe out with. As long as I can work this land at his side, that's what I want."

He straightened and looked out over the sagebrush behind them. "Sounds an awful lot like what your grandmother had to say when I asked her to come out here with me."

"Then it must be the right thing." She called another "get on!" to the cows, moving behind them.

"I'll still expect your help, Miss Rozzy." Papa Ed kicked his horse to come to a walk beside hers.

She moved Irene in closer, reaching out to take his hand and squeeze it, tough and coarse as the rope over her saddle horn. "Yes, Papa."

AGAINST HIS BETTER JUDGMENT, there was a bounce to Rafe's step when he came into his kitchen a few evenings later, and it wasn't until Jim asked, "Good day, boss?" that Rafe realized he was whistling as well.

He stopped, and guilt twinged in his stomach at his foreman's cautious tone. "I suppose so," he said, ruefully. Rozzy had sought him out every day to tag along while he worked. And he'd enjoyed having her company, so much that he found it more and more impossible to picture living without her—which he supposed was her exact intent. As well as showing him what she'd chosen—to not give up on any of her dreams. And against his better judgment, he found himself losing the will to fight for her to admit she needed him and nothing else.

"I hope you don't mind, boss," Mrs. Cowles said, coming into the kitchen. "I've told Jim he can join us for dinner. Mr. Pender paid my boys to help move Mrs. Pender's things, so it would be just us anyway."

Rafe smiled to himself as he finished drying his hands. "Sounds fine to me." Out of the corner of his eye, he noted the pink to his housekeeper's cheeks as she opened the oven and took out a pan of biscuits. He sauntered over to the table and took a seat at one end, eyeing Jim. "It would be quite convenient for me if I could set the two of you up in one house, instead of keeping up that shack for Jim."

"Mr. Adams, it's mighty unfair of you to tease Jim like that when you scolded him for the same thing." Mrs. Cowles slapped the biscuits on the table and turned away to retrieve more of the dinner from the stove.

Rafe cast Jim a look he hoped conveyed his apology for his short temper before. Jim nodded his understanding and gave him a half smile before turning to watch Mrs. Cowles busy herself at the stove, his expression smitten, to say the least.

"That's the perks of being the boss," Rafe teased.

"You leave Jim alone, boss." Mrs. Cowles wouldn't turn to look at him. "It's a lot to ask a man to take on three young boys when he's used to bachelorhood, and he doesn't need to be pressured by his employer to be hasty about that kind of decision."

"Do either of you intend for me to take part in the decision on whether I marry Adeline or not?" Jim asked dryly.

"What do you say, Jim?" Rafe enjoyed Mrs. Cowles's embarrassment more than he should as she tried to find things to keep her from the table and from looking at either of the men.

"I'll ask her on one condition," Jim said, turning to study Rafe. Mrs. Cowles froze mid stir but still didn't turn.

"What's that?" Rafe rested his elbows on the table and leaned into his hands.

"That you forgive Miss Rozzy."

Rafe gave a sigh and then a soft chuckle, shaking his head and leaning back. "I'm nigh headed that direction anyway, aren't I?" He lost all sense when it came to that woman.

"You ought to know that Adeline heard quite the rumor," Jim continued, resting his own elbows on the table and giving his boss a good, hard look.

"And that was?" The teasing mood around the table had dissipated, making Rafe wonder what gossip Little River society was spreading now. When he'd gone into town for his haircut the day before and stopped in at the general store, he'd heard that Tillie had spread gossip all over town that as soon as Rozzy quit this embarrassing show of pretending Rafe still loved her, he'd feel comfortable admitting that he and Tillie were going steady. One dance and he was going steady with the girl. He supposed this rumor was something like it.

And he deserved anything Tillie Van Doren spread about him. He'd warned Rozzy about Tillie's gossiping ways and, in his anger, hadn't followed that advice himself.

"That T.J. agreed to run the ranch when Big Ed retires," Jim seriously. Rafe froze and then furrowed his brows. "And that Miss Rozzy talked them both into it."

Rafe thought his heart might have stopped for a full minute. He hadn't thought it possible, especially the way she'd gone on about his stubbornness and how unfair and *patriarchal* it was. She hadn't missed a single opportunity during their work together the past few days to argue her points. To scold him for thinking she believed him anything like his father and that she only wanted the chance to work her land like he did the Double A. That if the situation were reversed, it would never cross her mind to think that he loved the Double A more than her—

despite all the sweat and tears he and his brothers had poured in to make sure they kept it in the family.

"Of course you'd *say* you'd choose me over your ranch," she'd retorted when he'd defended his stance. "You've never actually been in danger of losing it because you wanted to get married."

But despite sounding pretty sensible, she'd gone and given the Arrow C up anyway.

He blinked at Jim and tried to shake the surprise off. "Well," he choked out. He cleared his throat and stood. "I suppose it would be awful hard on Mrs. Cowles if I didn't give in—I would hate to thwart her happiness by being stubborn."

Mrs. Cowles brought over a pan of soup and set it on the table next to the biscuits. "I, in turn, care very much about Miss Rozzy's happiness," she said gently. "And how much it affects yours, boss."

Rafe arched an eyebrow. He hadn't stood a chance of turning that girl down in any case, not with the workforces of two ranches conspiring against him. "As I have gathered from Miss Rozzy's uncanny knowledge of where I have been working every day this week."

Mrs. Cowles shrugged and turned back for another pot. Jim laughed, and Rafe's mind eased on the score of the happiness of his friends. Truth be told, since breaking off his engagement, the tension in the house and between him and his foreman had pitched high, and that had meant a chill between him and his housekeeper as well. With his immediate family living far away, he considered Jim and Mrs. Cowles his closest thing to kin—besides Rozzy, of course. He had to admit that.

After Mrs. Cowles set the pot of gravy on the table but before she could move away, Jim took her hand in his and looked up at her. "Well, what do you say, Adeline? Will you marry me?"

Rafe interjected before the would-be-bride could answer. "If I'm to swallow so much of my pride and tell that hoyden she'd better not give her ranch up for me, you'd better propose right, Jim. Get down on one knee."

"Oh, come now, boss," Mrs. Cowles protested, but it held no weight as Jim slid out of his chair before she could finish.

He knelt down before Mrs. Cowles, taking her hand in his and sweeping his hat off with the other. "Will you marry me?" he repeated.

Mrs. Cowles put her other hand to her chest and then to her lips, and she nodded through what looked like a haze of tears. Jim stood, wrapping his arms around her and kissing her until she pushed him away and muttered something like, "Really, Jim, the boss is sitting right there."

Rafe smirked at Jim as she darted back to the stove, busying herself while she mopped up her face. Despite knowing that Mrs. Cowles would protest, he thought it a fine time to skip dinner and head over to the Arrow C. These two lovebirds deserved an evening alone anyway.

No one came to the door of the ranch house at the Arrow C right off, so Rafe let himself in and followed the voices coming from the parlor.

"It's mighty pretty, Miss Rozzy," Mrs. Hewitt said in a soft voice. "Such a shame."

"Don't sound so downhearted," Mrs. Pender replied in a cheerful voice. Rafe was surprised she didn't correct Mrs. Hewitt's use of Rozzy's nickname. "She's not quitting yet."

Rafe softened his steps as he approached, wondering how pretty he'd catch Miss Rozzy being and what kind of dress they went on and on about. Part of the pile of clothing T.J. had mentioned they'd brought back from Denver? T.J. had laughed about the dresses Mrs. Pender had insisted on buying that Rozzy would never wear in her life.

"Mother, why don't you have Mrs. Plummer make it over for you, and you can have a big party to celebrate you and Daddy being rightly married again?"

Mrs. Pender laughed. "What a thought, Rosaline."

Rafe made it to the doorway about the same time Mrs. Hewitt suggested, "We could dye it pink, Miss Rozzy. It would make a lovely evening dress if it wasn't white." And that's when he realized they were admiring the wedding dress Rozzy had asked Mrs. Plummer to make for her. Tillie Van Doren had no shame in recounting the gossip of it all when he'd taken her to that dance—after she'd made it sound like he'd invited her. Pain had twisted inside his gut at the story of Rozzy going straight to Mrs. Plummer when she returned from Denver, even though the whole town had heard by then that Rafe had called it all off.

"And who wouldn't?" Tillie had said, petting his arm as if he were a motherless calf. "The way she goes about, thinking you'll always trot along in her wake no matter what she does." He should have known better than to let Tillie Van Doren rile him up, but the words *had* struck home.

He stood quietly in the open doorway, listening to their discussion. He stared at the girl he'd loved since childhood, standing in the middle of the parlor with her mother and Mrs. Hewitt admiring her swaying back and forth in a dress that even a cowboy like Rafe could appreciate. Seeing her in it convinced him more than her dogging after him around his ranch that she meant to keep on him. It was right up there with her giving up the ranch for him, though it must have ripped her in two.

"Rafe!"

Her voice brought him out of his reverie, but he didn't stop staring. He hadn't regretted his promise to Jim to forgive her, especially after hearing what she'd done, but seeing her in that delicate dress with intricate embroidery and a veil cast over her head and drifting down her back made him sure glad he'd said it.

"Hope I'm not interrupting," he said, coming into the room, his eyes still all for Rozzy.

"We . . . I . . ." Rozzy fidgeted with the many layers of the frothy skirt before finally looking up to meet his gaze again. "Mrs. Hewitt wanted to see it," she said in a breathy voice.

He moved toward her, holding her gaze until he came close enough to reach out, cup her cheek in his hand, and bend over to kiss her gently. It thrilled him even more than the first one. He wasn't desperate to convince her of his love this time, only to thank her for hers. She lifted her arms to wrap them around his neck and let her fingers slide over the back of his head. He kept it short, though even one touch of her lips left him aching for more.

Soon enough. Soon enough.

"Oh, Rafe," she whispered when they broke apart. She stared up at him hopefully. "You'd better not be teasing me as some sort of revenge. Did you mean that kiss?"

He twisted one of the locks of hair that rested against her cheek and then brushed it back away from her face. "I meant it."

"I'll give it up for you, Rafe, I will. I've already worked it all out," she rushed on, her expression frantic. "You remember when I told you the ranch was sewn into my soul? Well, I think you must be a *part* of my soul, not even sewn in but made to be there. It's been awful thinking you might rip that part of me out."

He took her cheeks in his hands and pulled her to him again, kissing one cheek and then the other. "How is it that I've worked all my life to say things like that and I can't seem to get it half as good?" Yes, their souls had been made together. He'd lose no time in writing that down once he finished making up to her.

"Say something sweet right now." She leaned her forehead against his.

In the moment he took to gather up his thoughts, Rafe glanced around and realized that Mrs. Pender and Mrs. Hewitt had snuck out of the room, leaving them alone together. He thought of the poem he'd spent hours writing for her and tried to recall the things he'd written, but he couldn't remember any of it.

"I love you, Roz," he finally said. It was the sweetest thing he could think of, the most complete his thoughts had ever been, and not near enough to express the truth of his feelings.

She closed her eyes and smiled up at him, a look of absolute contentment smoothing her innocent features. "That's perfect." She laid her head on his shoulder and wrapped her arms around his chest. "And I love you."

"And secondly," he added, surprising her, "you had better not be fool enough to give this ranch to T.J. just because I said some silly things."

She reared her head back and stared at him with wide eyes. "Oh, you . . . you're as fickle as a Wyoming spring, aren't you!"

"All those years, you did teach *me* a thing or two."

She gasped and squeezed one of her hands between them to point a finger at him. "Now you listen here, Rafe Adams—"

But he didn't listen. He stopped up her tirade with another kiss, and he didn't mean to quit for a long time.

# CHAPTER 19

The church in Little River was packed to the brim with folks of all sorts there to witness a marriage they felt had been in the making for twenty years. As Rozzy stood at the door, gripping her father's arm and looking over all the guests, her eyes brimmed with tears. Even at the sight of Tillie and Bessie, who had really been her only choices for maids of honor. It was that or allow Irene to stand for her—which Reverend Watson refused.

Mrs. Plummer winked at her from the organ and began to play the "Wedding March," so Rozzy turned her attention to Rafe. He looked as smart as she had expected him to in his tux, with his broad shoulders squared and his hair combed to one side. Those blue eyes sparkled at her, and her heart soared at the thought that in a few minutes, he would be hers and they would keep on as best friends for the rest of their lives. She expected to ride the range with him until the day she died. It shouldn't surprise her that the man who had taught her all the important things about ranching was also the one who'd taught her about love.

They reached the end of the aisle, and Daddy prepared to hand her over to Rafe, his eyes glistening nearly as much as Mother's from where she sat in the front row with Papa Ed, Mrs. Hewitt, and Bert. Rozzy stood on her tiptoes and kissed Daddy on the cheek. She'd had dinner with him and Mother almost every night since they'd moved up to Rock Meadow, and as far as she could tell, her parents would be as blissfully happy as she was. They still argued about everything, but they enjoyed it much more now that they lived together again.

"I don't think you could have done better if I'd chosen myself, Roz," Daddy whispered as he held her close.

"But didn't you choose him?" she teased, squeezing her arms around him as best she could.

He chuckled. "I suppose I did—we all did, anyway." He held her hand out to Rafe, who took it with a choir-boy grin so large it could light up the whole room. As his rough hand closed around hers, the familiarity of him warmed her from the inside out until she thought she could light up the room too.

He let go long enough to lift the veil over her head, never taking his eyes from hers, and the happiness that had taken root that night he'd kissed her in this wedding dress grew by leaps and bounds. How could she have ever considered marrying for less than this—just to keep a silly old swath of sagebrush? To miss out on loving Rafe the rest of her life would have been unpardonable. To shackle Henry to her for the sake of her pride . . .

She and Rafe said their simple vows, hand in hand, neither looking away. And then Rafe Adams kissed her for the second time in that wedding dress, this time with an arm around her waist, holding her close. Everyone cheered while they kissed, and Daddy whistled loud enough to split the eardrums of those nearest him—earning himself a "now really, T.J.!" from Mother. All in all, it perfectly mirrored the celebration going on inside of Rozzy.

Later, after they'd had dinner at Rock Meadow with her family and all the guests and danced in the barn that half the town had helped raise on Daddy's new land, she and Rafe rode Rafe's horse from Rock Meadow to the Arrow C. Papa Ed planned to stay at Rock Meadow for a few weeks, making the Arrow C the home of the new couple. Daddy had laughed when he'd learned that Rafe wanted to follow in his footsteps and move into the ranch house at the Arrow C.

"Jim and Mrs. Cowles need somewhere to live," Rafe had said with a wink.

They were quiet as they rode, Rozzy sitting behind, her arms wrapped around Rafe's waist like she had ridden with him when she was a little girl. She smiled into the back of his shoulder and breathed him in.

Bert met them when they trotted into the yard, holding the reins while Rafe hopped off and then held out his hands for her to slide into. They kissed, smiles on their faces, before he lifted her into his arms and Bert's cheerful whistling faded into the night behind them.

Rafe carried her up the steps, and when they reached the door, he twisted the handle with the hand supporting her legs and stepped over the threshold. "Welcome home, Mrs. Adams," he said.

She put her hands around his neck, pulling him down to kiss her. "Too late, Rafe. I've been home since Reverend Watson pronounced me your wife."

"Well, I've got you beat." Rafe started up the stairs, Rozzy still held tightly in his arms. "I've been home here since the day you were born."

She grinned. "I've heard this story a hundred times," she whispered. "But tell me again how you held me just like I was yours."

He bypassed Rozzy's old room and headed for the larger bedroom that used to be Mother's—before that, Mother and Daddy's, and before that, Papa Ed's and Grandmother's. With a soft kick, he pushed the door open, but Rozzy had no intention of taking her eyes off him to gaze around the room Mother and Mrs. Hewitt had prepared for the newlyweds.

"You looked up at me just like that, Miss Rozzy," Rafe said in a soft voice. "Just like *I* was yours." He crossed the room in a couple strides and tossed her gently on the bed.

She laughed. "You gonna keep on about how long it took me to realize it?"

He leaned over her, kissing her forehead first. "All." He kissed her nose. "Your." He kissed her lips. "Life."

"Well, I suppose I deserve it," she said against his lips.

"You certainly do."

# ALSO BY RANEÉ S. CLARK

*Playing for Keeps*

*Double Play*

*Love, Jane*

*Meant for You*

The Love in Little River Series

*Roxy's Song*

*Dating Dru*

*Catching Coy*

*Hallie's Hero*

*June's Forever*

*Addy's Prince Charming*

*Battling Ben*

*Beneath the Bellemont Sky*

Coming September 2023

*A Lady's Promise*

Find all of Raneé S. Clark's books on Amazon.

https://amzn.to/2nUoXPC

You can listen to Love in Little River Audiobooks for FREE on YouTube

*Roxy's Song*

*Dating Dru*

*Catching Coy*

*Battling Ben*

https://bit.ly/RSCyoutube

# ABOUT THE AUTHOR

In a house overrun by boys, it shouldn't come as a surprise that Raneé loves football and enjoys watching (and playing!) other sports as well, like basketball and baseball. When she's not chauffeuring three busy boys to various activities (and sometimes while she is!), Raneé is either writing, reading (usually romance), obsessing over clothes in the form of her online boutique, or figuring out how to get a Crumbl cookie in rural Wyoming. When her real-life love interest can drag her away from imaginary worlds, she doesn't mind spending some time with him in the great outdoors that he loves.

You can find out more about Raneé's writing on Facebook and Instagram.

Made in the USA
Las Vegas, NV
13 February 2023

67442241R00089